W9-BBY-175

MATTEO STRUKUL

# The Ballad
# of Mila

*Translated by Marco Piva-Dittrich*
*and Allan Guthrie*

**EXHIBIT A**
An Angry Robot imprint
and a member of the Osprey Group

Lace Market House,
54-56 High Pavement,
Nottingham,
NG1 1HW
UK

AngryRobot/Osprey Publishing,
PO Box 3985,
New York,
NY 10185-3985
USA

www.exhibitabooks.com
A is for Azzurri!

First published in Italy in 2011
First published in English by Exhibit A in 2014

Cover photograph by Melissa Iannacce; design by Argh! Oxford
Set in Meridien and Futur Rough by Argh! Nottingham

Distributed in the United States by Random House, Inc., New York.

ISBN 978-1-90922-373-8
Ebook ISBN 978-1-90922-374-5

Printed in the United States of America

9 8 7 6 5 4 3 2 1

*For Silvia*

# Contents

# Matteo & Mila

AN INTRODUCTION BY VICTOR GISCHLER

This is an introduction. You're supposed to learn a little something about the author of this book from me – a fellow author.

So, of course, I need to talk about myself.

No, wait! Don't go. I'll make this quick and painless, and I promise it's relevant. Hang with me.

I first met Matteo Strukul face to face in the Turin airport after Air France lost my luggage. He was in charge of publicity for a small house in Italy which had published my first novel. I was a guest at a film and literature festival in the Alps, and Matteo had been charged with taking me around, arranging interviews and generally making sure I didn't get lost or fall down and hurt myself. What I learned about Matteo on that first promotional trip to Italy was that he was passionate and knowledgeable about all things hardboiled, noir, and pulp.

This fact became even more evident later when he helped co-found the Sugar Pulp movement in Italy, gathering together like-minded crime pulp aficionados. If you get a chance, hit their annual festival in Padova. Good fun. Matteo was later to head Revolver, Edizioni BD's crime fiction imprint. And now, as an author, you have a man who has seen the genre from just about every angle. Matteo Strukul is steeped in the hardboiled. He knows crime. He bleeds pulp.

And that's maybe why Mila and the other characters who populate her world are so rich and dynamic and... well... kick ass. The scenes crackle and pop and leap off the page. My favorite authors are intelligent people who refuse to misuse their intelligence by spending time trying to prove it to you, and Matteo doesn't have to. The work speaks for itself and knows what it's trying to do... and *does* it. Matteo has penned for us a grand ballet of blood, an opera of violence, a ballad of badassery. A smart novel, yes, but not a look-how-smart-I-am novel, and that is where

Matteo – and indeed the entire genre – wins. Pulp is at its best when it strips away pretension and grabs you by the balls. I should have said that simpler and sooner.

*The Ballad of Mila* owns your balls, man.

And isn't that what we all want from our pulp crime fiction? A ball-grabber?

And while you or I may have visited Padova or other Italian cities as tourists, it's quite doubtful you've experienced it the way you will in *The Ballad of Mila*. Matteo has shown me Italy with new eyes, a native's eyes. As an American crime writer, I sometimes fall into the trap of thinking we have a lock on cities with gritty underbellies (and down here in Louisiana, swamps filled with seedy backwoodsy types) but Matteo illustrates with eerie authenticity that you might think of Italy as a country with some of the best food and wine in the world, but you can still get killed in a New York Minute (a Venice minute?) if you wander down the wrong dark alley. Matteo's sense of place is one of the novel's great strengths.

But the crowning achievement, of course, is Mila herself. There is something about a beautiful woman with a sword that simply *works*. And while it's certainly possible that this archetype might let us down in the hands of an author with lesser skills, I am delighted to report that is *not* the case here. Matteo's expert sense of pace and character allows Mila to stretch her bloody, vengeful wings and fly through the pages of this scorching novel.

Since that first trip, I've been back to Italy a number of times. (Gischler is talking about himself again!) But now, I don't think of Matteo as the guy who keeps me from falling over myself (although he still does that). I think of him as a friend… and now as a brother author. While in Italy, during interviews arranged by Matteo, I would often be asked the following question: "What Italian authors do you read?" Embarrassingly, the answer at the time was not very damn many. The truth is that a lot more English fiction is translated into Italian than vice versa. So it is no small compliment to Matteo that Exhibit A would select *The Ballad of Mila* to lead what will hopefully be a charge of excellent crime fiction going back in the other direction toward America. Italy could do a lot worse than to make Matteo Strukul the face of Italian pulp crime.

So. There. An introduction. If you were smart, you skipped over this to dive into Matteo's excellent novel. If not, don't fret. There's still time.

Turn the page.
Hurry.

*Victor Gischler*
*December 2, 2013*

# The Ballad of Mila

"Chinese mafia a real danger in Padua; Carlo Mastelloni, the Venice District Attorney, raises awareness."

IL MATTINO DI PADOVA, *19 October 2010*

# 0

Chen narrowed his eyes: two thin cracks onto which red liquid dripped. Blood was falling from deep cuts in his forehead, a veil that blurred his vision.

The promise of death.

Zhang, the guy standing in front of him, was the one who had inflicted the wound.

Zhang looked at him, smiling, holding a butterfly knife, its blade red with Chen's blood. Zhang burst out in nervous laughter while taking in all the details of the little shop.

He smelled the spices, moved his gaze to the coloured boxes and cans of food. Packets of Lungkow noodles with their bright red dragons;

the yellows and reds of Quick Cooking; grey boxes of flour for making Salapao steamed buns; the transparent packaging of the Wai Wai rice noodles and the Yan Long, made from sweet potatoes.

He smiled once again, satisfied. As if all those things belonged to him. He licked his upper lip, a merciless light in his eyes.

"Got yourself a really nice shop, Chen, don't you?"

"Ye... Yes..."

Zhang flicked the double handle of the butterfly knife again. The short blade flew through the air like a hungry tongue, swinging fast in a macabre, shining dance. He seemed to want to buy time before getting down to business. He took all the time he needed, making sure that fear seized the very bones of the small, skinny man in front of him.

On the Formica counter where Chen had set up the cash register and jars of brightly coloured candies, there was a bunch of red sword lilies. Their long stems formed a green lozenge. Their petals, strong and thick, expelled a strong perfume, a pungent fragrance.

"Have you seen them?" asked Zhang, lifting his chin and indicating the lilies with a simple movement.

"Yes..." whispered Chen in a weak voice.

"You know what they mean, don't you?"

"Sword..."

"Yes, sword and blood. Death, you ungrateful bastard! It's futile to try to avoid my rage and the revenge of your lord, Guo Xiaoping, the Dragon Head of the Talking Daggers! Xin and Lao both know you have to die."

Xin and Lao, crew-cut and specs, had just tied his hands behind his back. Slices of the shop's neon lighting bounced off the dark lenses partially hiding their eyes. But, still, Chen could feel their gaze digging into his face.

Zhang exhaled through his nose. "And all because you're late with your payments again this month," he told him. "Do you want to keep what you're earning, thanks to my uncle? You become greedy, Chen? Do we need to ask your permission to have what you owe us, you little freshwater crab?"

Chen's mouth was sealed, fear holding his words in. He lowered his eyes. Silent tears made their way through the blood and ran down his cheeks, his thin face, his high cheekbones.

"I don't think I heard you," prompted Zhang.

"Of course, Guo doesn't need to ask for what he's owed..."

"Ah, that's better," sighed Zhang. "Seems you're not as stupid as you'd like us to believe."

He walked to the colourful tins of Shiitake-Poku mushrooms and the green cans of Aroy-D bamboo shoots. Moved the knife to his left hand and his right swept across the shelves.

A cascade of tins crashed onto the floor. A sudden, deafening noise. Zhang booted the cans away.

He turned back towards Chen.

"You want to keep everything for yourself, right? Damn you! You forgot, my uncle sees everything you do. Guo Xiaoping is the Mountain Master. And he sent me as a reminder. I treat infected wounds. The Talking Daggers are like the body of a great dragon. A body can't work unless each limb, each organ, each atom does exactly what nature instructs it to do. Chen, your nature is to pay Guo what you owe him."

As he spoke, Zhang got closer. He smiled a crazy, wide grin. Whirled the knife in front of the old man's face, then quickly stuck him in the stomach.

The blade went deep. Four times. It entered the flesh, ripped, and came out dripping, ready to bite and tear again.

Since his hands were tied, Chen couldn't even clasp them to his stomach. He saw his innards leaking out, unable to do anything, his eyes nearly popping out with the pain. His legs slowly gave way. Xin and Lao helped him down as he slumped to the ground. He slithered quietly, in a pool of blood and inner organs.

"Ew! Disgusting…" hissed Zhang. "You look like a gutted fish! And all because you wouldn't listen to us, you stupid greedy bastard!" Then he raised his eyes, stared at Xin and Lao.

"Clean everything up. Tomorrow this shithole of a shop will have a new owner."

"What'll we do with the corpse?" asked Xin.

"I saw a bathroom in the back. Chop him up in the tub, then call my uncle. He'll give you an address. Pack the pieces of the old man up in plastic bags, put them in the car boot and drive there. Get in through the gate and drop everything in the cellar. Stuff all the pieces in the furnace at the end of the hall and burn everything. Here's the keys. I'll go check on that idiot, Longhin. I gave my word he's good and I can't afford him to fail. My honour's at stake."

While Xin and Lao dragged Chen's body towards the bathroom, Zhang produced a red handkerchief from his pocket and carefully wiped the blade of his butterfly. He did a thorough job. Folded the blade back with a flick of his wrist and slid it into the pocket of his dark grey trousers, then left the minimarket with an elegant stride.

Only after he was gone, did Chen finally die.

# 1

It was really cold.

Piles of dirty snow along the road. Mounds of grey stretching all the way along.

Severino Pierobon – known as Two Hundred because the horses he bet on usually gave up in the last two hundred metres – arrived at Le Padovanelle racetrack in his yellow Citroën C2. As usual, he had no trouble finding somewhere to park. Horse-racing was a dying sport, and betting was a daydream for nostalgics.

He'd done everything thoroughly, as usual. Studied all the horses: the results of the latest races, the positions, what the experts said.

Horse racing was important to him. It had been

in his blood since he was a kid, when he'd tagged along with his grandpa to Le Padovanelle. Since then, he'd followed the same ritual each and every week. Sometimes he won, but never anything big; just enough to go home with a tray of pastries. He'd stuff himself with them, alone in his kitchen; he ate himself silly because he loved cakes, even though he was supposed to be taking care of himself, having been diagnosed with diabetes.

Severino Pierobon didn't smoke and didn't have sex. He drank grappa and ate cakes. That was it. He was fifty and had no intention of reaching ninety if it meant eating vegetables, cereal and salad. He'd rather die young.

In his hand was a really sweet cappuccino in a plastic cup.

He knew he needed to trust in God. Or whoever. Despite his immense experience he had never been able to devise a winning system: there were far too many variables. But that feeling of uncertainty, of craziness, was exactly what pushed him to keep betting. A drunken feeling, at least as strong as the hope that grabbed him by the throat as soon as he saw the sulkies dashing from the starting line.

He scratched his unkempt beard, thinking that it was the first time he'd bet on a Monday. It had never been that cold in Padua, and the thick snow had caused the Saturday races to be postponed a couple of days.

He passed some time at the bar, then made a stop at the toilets. Suddenly he realised that he had to get a move on. He entered the door to the stands and reached the track-side railing the very moment Gastone Pink broke away from the others. But he'd broken away too early. He'd been hoping to see something now, for once, but no chance: that small, fast horse, chocolate-dark, had reached Bon Vivant first, then taken the lead.

Gastone Pink couldn't help it, it was its nature: he always took the lead early. But he could never hold on to it. That was his biggest weakness. Everybody knew this, even Two Hundred. That's why Alberto Leoni, the driver, was bobbing about in his sulky trying to get Gastone Pink to stay in the lead till the end, for once.

Severino Pierobon shook his head.

Angrily, he threw his crumpled copy of *Trot & Turf* to the ground. Kept watching that damned four-legged chunk of chocolate getting ready to steam on towards the finishing post. He still hoped, in his heart, that maybe Gastone Pink had enough in the tank to crush his opponents this time.

Around him, the Le Padovanelle regulars stared in silence at those twelve shining coats speeding along the sandy track. It was always a beautiful sight, seeing them in action, proud, fast, their hooves beating the rhythm of the challenge.

The chill was relentless. The cold air cut into faces, clouds twisting like white curls of fat in the blue frying pan of the sky.

"Gastone Pink'll fade before the end," someone said. "He's not mature enough yet and Leoni's unable to hold him back. Too bad, he's a really nice horse."

Casual words, comments made just to annoy. Severino Pierobon was already visualising his umpteenth crushing defeat.

But horse racing is not a sport like any other. Believe it or not, it never matches your expectations. And Severino Pierobon, aka Two Hundred, knew that.

Gastone Pink was staying in front. He wasn't tiring. Maybe he'd made an exception, just this once, and was going to hold on. A satisfied grin slowly started to appear on Severino's face.

The seconds passed. Two Hundred felt them rolling through his head. With each one, the image of his horse winning the race became less and less unreal.

The little bay kept eating up the ground with his strong, stocky legs, and he seemed to be enjoying it. He was giving his best and had a decent advantage, ten metres or so. He kept knocking back the advances of the eleven dark devils trying to catch up with him, and ploughed straight ahead, as if on drugs, ignoring the silly humans who had suddenly started shouting. His legs brushed through the air without breaking pace and – unbelievably – Gastone Pink stretched even further ahead.

From his sulky, Alberto Leoni was encouraging him, shouting something nobody could understand. The horse was tearing along like a beauty.

Two Hundred heard himself shouting "Go, go, you little bastard!", the words banging against his clenched teeth, his clenched jaw.

Then... then something happened which he really didn't want to see: a dark, muscular mare, big as an oil tanker, emerged from the chasing group. Two Hundred started to worry. His enthusiasm wavered; he felt a hard, metallic pain in his stomach, held his breath. Stood still, not moving, as if he didn't want to tilt the delicate balance that might bring his horse an unexpected victory.

"Imperatrice will swallow Gastone Pink whole," said a fat, pockmarked woman wearing a commodious coat with a fake fur collar.

But Severino Pierobon decided not to give up. Like Gastone Pink.

"He's going to do it. He's going to do it, for fuck's sake!" he shouted, his voice betraying his tension.

Imperatrice was catching up at the speed of light; she was swallowing the little horse whole exactly like that damn lard-ass had prophesied, but Gastone Pink was still holding onto the lead.

"Come on, come on, don't give up, don't let that big beast catch up, hold on!"

Both horses hit the last two hundred metres. Two Hundred started getting excited; it was nearly over. The frustration that had been building up for years now became electric enthusiasm, a wave of energy strong enough to reach the horse, or at least Severino Pierobon hoped so.

And maybe that was exactly what happened. Gastone Pink kept going even though that furious lioness behind him was getting closer and closer. But he kept the lead with his precision pacing, as beautiful as the sun that had just come out from behind the clouds to watch him. And, with a thoroughly gutsy display, not only did he maintain his advantage but he sped up and won.

Shutting up all those who had said he couldn't do it, including the pockmarked lard-ass. And leaving Two Hundred's jaw gaping next to the railing, blowing white steam into the air of that winter afternoon.

Thanks to that crazy little bay horse, he had finally won a four-horse accumulator. To be precise, he had guessed the exact finishing positions of the first four horses. But, even though anyone would have guessed that Imperatrice, Otto Nix and Capitan Germal would come home in the top positions, nobody would have bet a single cent on Gastone Pink.

That combination was worth 26,645 euros. Just saying.

Severino Pierobon started stroking his chin.

Heckler & Koch USP Tactical, left-handed threaded barrel. Knight's Armament Company silencer. A small gun, perfect for what he needed to do.

He knew he would use it. Because he had to go all the way. Refusing would be akin to giving up, and giving up is the best advantage you can give your enemy. That's what he'd been told by his boss, Guo Xiaoping, who was quoting Master Kongzi. Guo was a short, mean Chinaman, pointy teeth, the leader of a gang of Asians that had been spreading across the Veneto region.

He had given him fifteen thousand euros, cash, no problem.

As if he had been a short – and yellow – brother of Rockefeller.

His targets: Marco and Mirco Galesso. Twins from Verona, chartered accountants. They recycled the money earned by the Pagnan family, major league players in the local criminal underworld, through their drugs and prostitution rackets. The Galesso brothers laundered it, investing it in perfectly legal activities through a chain of companies strategically located in tax havens. From there they transferred it all over the place, following the ebbs and flows of the global market. Finally, they hid the money in secret accounts in Luxembourg or the Channel Islands, with such speed and secrecy that the Customs and Excise Police had no fucking idea.

Guo Xiaoping planned to kick the Pagnan family in the ass, just to show that he was serious. He planned to overpower the Italians and wanted to send them a message: *Today I am killing your accountants. Tomorrow, if I want to, I will kill you. And my hired gun is one of your own men, Ottorino Longhin.*

Ottorino Longhin was in his car, where he could keep an eye on the service station toilets without being seen. He was busy screwing the silencer onto the barrel of his Heckler & Koch, only one thought in mind: he mustn't fail. The Chinaman had been very clear about that. Hadn't left him any options.

But as time passed, he felt less and less sure of himself. He kept repeating in his head what he needed to do: stick a card saying "Out of Order" on the toilet door; get in; hide in one of the stalls; wait for those two idiots; shoot them both in the back of the head, twice; get out leaving the card where it was; cross the parking lot; climb into his black BMW 120; get the fuck out of there.

That was, ideally, what he would do. He had repeated it to himself thirty-seven times that afternoon already.

Thirty-seven, he'd counted them.

And then? Then he'd get a further fifteen thousand euros, a new passport and a flight to Martinica. His wife? An old, fat, acne-scarred bitch addicted to horse racing. That was over. His kids? Two petty criminals who'd sucked his life away like leeches. Over with them too. His old life? Over, as well.

The Pagnan family? No longer any of his business. Ten years of hard, dirty work for that bunch of retards. Husband, wife, their sons, the usual family of distrustful, greedy people from Veneto, always busy pillaging their family business and thus forcing him to produce mountains of cash courtesy of a host of shady activities.

Thus Ottorino Longhin decided to become a turncoat. A local screwing over another local.

Typical. All to the advantage of the Chinks. As if those fucking Slant-Eyes needed help putting the already-troubled Italian north-east in a difficult position. The economic miracle had become a mere shadow of its past self. Fucking immigrants, Longhin thought. But they paid well. Cash. And he was already in up to his neck.

So, thank you and goodbye.

But first he needed to kill Marco and Mirco Galesso.

He saw them coming in. Fat, reeking of smoke, clumsy, even more so than usual thanks to their identical grey suits, at least one size too small. Two fucking sacks of shit decorated with Armani glasses with perfectly round frames. Ottorino, he was thin as a rake, his face sunken by poverty, sharp as a knife. He would walk in and blow them away. Just give them time to grab hold of their cocks and then he'd finish them off. He waited a little longer, reminding himself that this was his last hurdle before he could leave his old life behind.

The Galesso twins walked into the toilets, stood in front of the urinals and started chatting.

"You prepared the sauté sauce?" said Mirco.

"Hey, I did everything just right," replied Marco.

"Oil, onions, roasted the rice properly...?" continued the former.

"I just told you I did, for fuck's sake! And I added the broth and the Amarone."

"Parmesan to make everything creamier?"

"Christ, Mirco, you really think I'm an idiot? I followed the recipe step by step."

"There's nothing quite like risotto, remember!"

"Actually there's at least one thing: did you see that fucking hot piece of skirt you just bumped into?"

"What piece of skirt?"

"Christ, are you that stupid? The one with a Negro hairdo, the huge boobs and the leather trousers outlining that sweet ass!"

"Ah, that one... right, right, don't get upset. Of course I saw her."

"Christ Almighty, sometimes I wonder if you're a queer."

"Hey, no woman ever complained. God's gift between the sheets, me..."

"Yep, of course you are! You're standing here jerking off over a risotto. You realise that's not normal?"

"These things need to be done carefully!"

"Yeah, whatever. Me, I like pussy."

"What's up with you? I just asked how you prepared the risotto. No need to insult me!"

"Hm. Right, OK, let me take a piss in peace."

And as he was saying "peace" the door to the toilets opened. Ottorino Longhin appeared like a puppet in a theatre.

He smiled as they opened their mouths. Then without even taking aim, he emptied the magazine of the Heckler & Koch.

T*umpf, tumpf, tumpf.*

*Tumpf, tumpf, tumpf.*

Within four seconds, Marco and Mirco were human jam. They crumpled onto the floor, which was already soaked with their blood.

Ottorino Longhin had gone a little over the top. But it was all good. He removed the empty magazine and dug out a new one from his leather jacket. Now he needed to get out and scarper at the speed of light.

Severino Pierobon stopped at the Limenella Nord service station.

Even though he'd already gone at the racetrack, he needed to take a leak. Urgently. Maybe it's the adrenalin kicking in after the win, he thought.

As soon as he'd parked he saw a patrol car. A couple of cars had crashed in the parking lot and their owners had called the police.

Whatever. He closed the door of his Citroën

and ran towards the toilets. He was running hard; he was afraid he'd burst. The chill didn't help. It was late January, the coldest time of the year; his full bladder and the cold air formed a deadly alliance against his urinary tract.

On the wooden toilet door, the paint flaking, he saw a sign saying "Out of Order". But he was fucked if he was going to piss his pants. Without thinking twice he headed towards the door, which opened that very instant.

Severino's impetus made him crash into a man who was hurriedly barging out. He found himself grabbing him and, a second later, lying on the tiled floor.

"Fuck!" shouted Longhin, venting his frustration at finding himself in the arms of the living dynamo that had crashed into him. Now they were swimming together in the Galesso twins' blood.

"Shit!" shouted Two Hundred as soon as he saw the slaughterhouse in which the two bodies – torn apart by bullets – were floating. He saw splatters of blood all around. Felt like throwing up. Brought a hand to his mouth to hold back a retch and tried to stand up, but his old Clarks skidded in the blood and he lost his balance. He managed to stand up and make his way to the door, filled with a terror that held him by the throat. He felt a warm liquid trickle down his legs.

He was pissing himself.

Longhin saw the man dash towards the door. He dashed after him.

When Longhin and Two Hundred burst out into the parking lot one after another, the former shouting with his eyes bulging out of their sockets and the latter's face white with fear, they ended up about fifty yards from where the policemen stood, completing their reports.

One of them heard shouts and turned around. Just in time to see Longhin raise his arm, aim and fire.

*Tumpf.*

Two Hundred felt a sharp pain in his thigh. Suddenly his legs became as steady as cake mixture. He crashed to the ground, bleating like a wounded calf.

Before the policeman could utter a word, Longhin was standing over Severino, aiming the Heckler & Koch at his head.

"Don't move or I'll put a hole in his brain," he shouted at the cop.

"Put the gun down" the cop replied as he unholstered a .9 Beretta.

"Don't shoot or he'll kill me!" shouted Two Hundred just to make his presence known. Sure his opinion would have some weight in the current situation.

The situation was: bad guys, one hundred points. Good guys, nil. Victims, exact score unknown, but pretty low.

Anyone within twenty yards seemed to realise that it was not a movie set. Guns, shots, blood: all real.

After a few moments in which silence froze time, men, women and children started shouting in unison, as if they had arranged it, and started running around like headless chickens.

The policemen didn't move.

Two Hundred was shivering. The blood oozing from his right thigh had turned his jeans dark red.

Not knowing what to do next, Longhin opted for some sound effects. He thought that covering the screams of terror with the roar of his gun might be a good idea. He removed the silencer and started shooting.

*Bang, bang.*

*Bang, bang.*

*Bang, bang.*

A round of lead sweets for all, windscreen blown to pieces like broken mirrors, tyres hissing as they collapsed. Amidst all the bullets and screaming, Longhin grabbed his bleeding hostage by the neck and walked towards the small shop in the service station.

• • •

Inside the shop, seven people.

A cashier, her head awash with platinum blonde curls as if someone had poured a tray of cannelloni over her. An elderly German couple, the man skinny and nervous with pale blue eyes, the woman fat, as big as an aircraft carrier, but with a charming shepherdess-like face. Two children, a boy and a girl, holding hands, the former with a humungous bubble of snot hanging from his nose. A guy with sleek hair, muscular under a Jacquard-style sweater.

And her.

A bombshell: medium height, red dreadlocked hair, green eyes; sheathed in leather trousers and a tight jacket perfectly highlighting her curves. Breathtakingly hot.

On the left a small table covered in coffee cups, empty glasses, two-day old croissants.

Longhin loaded a new magazine. Then he did something that some might consider obvious.

And quite cruel.

He fired.

A bullet from his Heckler & Koch hit the huge German woman in the middle of her vast belly.

Her husband shouted *"Scheisse!"* and used his hands to try to stop the blood that was flowing from his wife's gut as if a pump was sucking it out of a ship's hold.

Two Hundred stared at the scene, numbed by his blood loss. His jeans, wet with blood and piss, were sticking to his leg.

The children were crying.

The German man kept spitting words in a harsh, dark accent, pretty much the same noise an anvil would make spin-drying in a washing machine.

The muscular guy was hiding behind the ice cream fridge.

The cashier was praying, "Please, sir, don't hurt me."

"Down on your bellies!" screamed Longhin. "And nobody do anything stupid or you'll find yourself with an extra hole in you, big as the one I put in the fat woman."

"She needz a doctor or she vill die!" said the German.

"Shut up or I'll kill you, you fucking Nazi."

As everyone went down, the red-haired woman walked towards Longhin and Pierobon. Her green eyes looked like Indian jade; they didn't betray any nervousness, any fear.

"The fuck's up with you?" Longhin shouted at her. "You a Rasta looking for trouble?"

She didn't reply. Kept walking straight ahead, stopped right in front of Longhin, put on a pair of glasses with weird yellow-tinted lenses and opened the front of her jacket to display a white T-shirt.

On her T-shirt, "Girls kick ass".

"If I lie on the ground I'll get my T-shirt dirty, and I'm particularly fond of it," said the girl, her mouth stretching into a grin that meant trouble.

"Are you taking the piss? I'll give your throat a lead tattoo!"

"With a water pistol?" she asked, shaking her head as if to tell him off. "You're going to get hurt. Bad."

Outside, a loudhailer started to croak.

"Drop your weapon and come out with your hands up," the voice of a policeman said.

Longhin kept his gun trained on the side of Two Hundred's temple, Two Hundred who couldn't feel his right leg and was leaning heavily on the counter behind which the cashier was obediently lying on the floor.

The two Germans were silent. Mr Muscle, as motionless as a cowhide rug, was also on the floor, behind the ice cream fridge.

The children were watching the scene unfold, also from a prone position.

The girl stopped waiting.

She planted her feet on the ground and head-butted Longhin. She hit him hard, as if she was hammering a nail into a tree trunk. The blow gained power as it struck. There was a noise like a stick hitting an empty trunk.

Longhin moaned softly; maybe he was trying to scream.

He staggered backwards.

She lunged forward and hit him with her right hand, a chop to the throat, the natural conclusion of a fluid, seamless motion. She had practiced that move thousands of times until it flowed perfectly.

Longhin struggled to breathe. He muttered something, his hands covering his face. The blood started oozing down his chin, down his neck.

The Red Fury jumped in the air and kicked him smack in the groin. Ottorino fell to his knees then crumpled to the floor like a puppet broken by a moody child. She didn't waste any time. Took the Heckler & Koch, grabbed him by the hair and dragged him outside like a pig's carcass.

She dropped him at the feet of the policeman holding the loudhailer. He had been watching the scene, wide-eyed.

"Here you go," said the girl.

"Thank you," replied the man.

Behind them, the flashing lights of ambulances and squad cars.

Two Hundred dragged himself out of the small shop, limping heavily.

He looked at the policemen. "In the toilets…"

he started babbling, "…a massacre… in there. And a woman too… in the shop…"

Then he looked at the beautiful woman with the red dreadlocks who was smiling at him.

"I don't know what to say," he whispered.

"Don't worry, there's nothing to say," she replied. "Everything's fine."

They walked together towards the ambulance.

Two Hundred took his winning ticket from his pocket. It was red, blood red.

"What's your name?"

"Mila."

"Here you go, Mila."

"No, thanks. I don't like betting on the horses. I prefer motor racing."

"But this is a winning ticket!"

She looked at him coolly and told him, "So am I."

# 2

Great.

She had given her witness testimony to the police.

She was holding the keys of the twins' car. Leaving the toilets earlier she had seen them and had "accidentally" bumped into one of them, taking the keys out of his pocket; that idiot hadn't even realised it. Easier than stealing candy from a kid. Then she'd saved the people in the small shop. So she was coming out of it completely unscathed.

All perfect.

The Mercedes C30 shone in the sun like a shark beneath the waves.

She opened the boot: two black leather cases.

Inside the first: wads of cash, at least two hundred banknotes in each brick. Five-hundred euro notes. A lot of money.

Inside the second: the same.

She closed the cases and the boot. Got into the car and drove it towards the service station exit. A few yards away the police had cordoned off the area and scene of crime officers were now gathering all the usual evidence.

Zhang Wen was holding his mobile phone. He had just slid a couple of green pills under his tongue.

Zhang personally managed the trafficking of those little pills through a network of very young pushers. That horse tranquiliser was doing well on the Veneto market. At twenty euros per pill, it helped him make a lot of money.

After visiting Chen's minimarket, he'd changed his clothes. He always had at least one spare suit in his car, in a sealed plastic bag from the dry cleaner's.

While he waited, he found a way to admire himself in the flat surface of a window. He was wearing a tailor-made dark blue suit. Beneath it a pearl-coloured tie and a white shirt. On top, a black jacket that went down to his ankles.

Reflective shades and a crew cut completed the image.

He had been swallowing the last sip of a watered-down iced Coke from the pedestrian bridge over the motorway at the Limenella Nord service station, when he finally saw the Mercedes leave the parking lot.

He dashed towards his Porsche Cayenne. Back in the car again, he dialled the number he knew he had to call and started following the girl. After the usual sixteen rings, Guo Xiaoping picked up.

"I'm listening."

"We're screwed," said Zhang, and snorted. He was annoyed that his uncle was speaking Italian to him. They were Chinese, from Wenzhou. Why the fuck did they need to use that barbaric language? Yes, of course, his uncle had told him that it was very useful to learn the language of their enemy, that doing so gave them a precious advantage. They had discussed it several times, and there had been no way to change Guo's mind.

"Why?"

"The police have Longhin! Alive."

"How?"

"Some girl beat him to a pulp and delivered him to them."

"What about the accountants?"

"He killed them."

"So the damage is minor. We need to get rid of Longhin. And the girl. Nobody can be allowed to think they can make me a fool out of me by treating my men like idiots."

"Even if they are big polenta to the Italian north-east?"

"*From* the Italian north-east," Guo corrected. He was a precise man, he loved discipline and grammar and couldn't stand the fact that his nephew kept using the wrong prepositions after so many years.

"Of, from, to… the Italian north-east, it's all the same!"

"No," Guo spat, nearly choking. "It is not all the same. You need to learn! You promised!"

"Promised, promised… In the meantime I'm learning to pronounce R rather than L. And I hate you talking to me this way. You're my uncle after all, and you owe me some respect!" Zhang pronounced the R in "respect" like an angry Spaniard. Perfectly enunciated.

"Right. Back to the matter in hand. Anything else you need to tell me?"

"Yes."

"I'm listening."

"The girl left with the Merc."

"And you didn't follow her?"

"I'm fifty yards behind her, on the motorway."

"Good. Find out where she's going."

"OK."

"Where did they take Longhin?"

"Padua hospital."

"Are you sure?"

"Yes uncle, trust me."

"Good! So, while you're following that girl, call Zou Kai and tell him to go to the Padua hospital with some of his guys. We need to eliminate Longhin from the equation before Pagnan's men grab him. The less they know about him selling out, the better for us. We need to hang onto the surprise factor. And even if Pagnan's men fail, that idiot might tell the police something. So we need to be fast."

"I agree, uncle."

"Right, that's all from me."

"Same here."

In the relaxation room of his house, Guo Xiaoping shook his head. His nephew was still far from adept at pronouncing the Italian language. An amateur, he told himself. Guo strongly believed that it was important to perfect the pronunciation. It was necessary to show he had integrated completely in order to screw up those ignorant nationalists all the more effectively.

In two days, he was taking part in a debate about cultural integration. He had been invited by the president of the provincial SME confederation, a man who considered Guo a rare example of a non-European entrepreneur who had integrated so well into the social fabric that he had become an asset to the local economy.

Guo really wanted to make a good impression. And he was afraid his nephew would do something stupid. He had to make sure Zhang stayed at home, but unfortunately he was sure that the young man would do everything he could to be there.

Guo snorted.

Then he thought back at how he had devised his speech. He planned to start from an historical perspective, explaining how, century after century, the Chinese had always shown respect and gratitude towards the people who had welcomed them. He'd thought of several excellent examples, one of which was about the Chinese workers who helped build the American railroad, sleeper after sleeper, from the east coast to the west.

He felt that he could do a really good job and impress the president, thus becoming a player. And thereby eliminating any doubts they might still harbour about him.

If only his stupid nephew, that dumb-ass loose cannon, would behave himself.

The Mercedes was running like a dream.

The clouds had cleared.

Mila felt like a bird in spring.

She had left the motorway, rejoined it in the opposite direction and was now heading for Marco Polo airport outside Venice.

She planned to leave one of the two cases in a left luggage locker before taking the next step. But first she needed to buy a big holdall, a tennis bag maybe, to put the cases in. Just to avoid entering the airport looking like someone who'd stolen a couple of million euros.

Soon both the Chinese and the locals would realise that they were being fucked with. Then she'd turn them against each other and dice them, like mozzarella on a pizza. Spring cleaning. She was already dreaming of having to pick them up with a spoon.

The Porsche Cayenne kept following her.

It had to be a total idiot behind the wheel. A car like that was as noticeable as a turd in a bowl of soup.

Mila drove at a steady speed until the motorway ended in Mestre, then she suddenly turned and took the ramp towards Porto

Marghera. The Porsche was left behind and disappeared from sight.

After a couple of turns she got to the town centre. She parked the Mercedes in front of a sport shop. A few minutes later she came out with a Nike tennis bag. She opened the boot and put one of the cases in the bag.

She got back into the car and drove to the airport.

The Porsche, which had reappeared meanwhile, parked a short distance behind her.

Mila entered the arrivals terminal and walked to the left luggage area. She picked a locker at random and put her bag inside. Then added the key to her keyring to make it look inconspicuous.

She went back to the motorway, following the same road she had taken earlier to get there. She left the motorway at Padua West and drove the A road towards Castelfranco Veneto until she reached Vigodarzere. Once she had reached Saletto she got to a residential area.

She parked the Mercedes in front of a small, semi-detached house.

She grabbed the remaining case from the boot and entered her home.

She flung off her clothes and left them on the floor, got to the bathroom and entered the shower, imagining the sensation of the hot water on her skin. She wanted to pamper herself a little before having dinner, but most of all she wanted to free her mind. She had a pretty challenging meeting coming up and wanted to be fully fit for it.

After fifteen minutes of what seemed to her a sweet anti-stress therapy, she left the shower and wrapped herself in a white honeycomb robe.

She went to her shiny kitchen. Washed some strawberries and prepared a smoothie. She smiled; her smile was sweet and cruel at the same time.

Zhang Wen had not understood one single iota of what was going on.

After the call with his uncle, he had followed the girl, but lost her near the Porto Marghera exit. He left the motorway and reached the town, where he had driven around aimlessly until he spotted her leaving a sports shop. Then he followed her, still at a distance, to the short stay parking lot of Marco Polo airport. There he remained in the car, hoping he wouldn't have to wait for long. After about fifteen minutes he saw her walk back to the Mercedes without her sports bag.

Maybe she had delivered it to someone inside the airport, or she'd left it in a locker. He couldn't think of any alternatives. But it looked dodgy. Decidedly dodgy. If that girl was driving the car belonging to Pagnan's accountants, then that bag contained either money or sensitive documents. Anyway, he was close to deciding to put an end to wandering around Veneto after her. He was planning on squeezing all the information he could out of her before putting a couple of bullets in her head and bye bye baby.

Zhang followed the Mercedes again. He parked his Porsche Cayenne half a block after the pretty house the redhead had walked into.

Only then he remembered that he was supposed to call Zou Kai and send him to the Padua hospital to kill Longhin. Shit, he'd fucked up. Guo would murder him.

With trembling hands, he called Zou Kai's mobile. After fourteen rings, Zou picked up. Zhang told him what had happened at the service station. The other man understood immediately that there was a fuck-ton of trouble on its way. He said he would call a couple of friends and then leave immediately, but he was not exactly in the area and it would take him a while to get there. Zhang shouted that he needed to be fast.

He ended the call with the unpleasant feeling of having a dirty conscience.

Immediately afterwards, he phoned Xan Jingyu

and asked him to come over, along with Wu Jingjing. He had decided to call for help: after having seen the girl at work, he would rather avoid any further trouble.

As he waited, he got out of the car to stretch his legs. He checked the two Walther PPK 7.65s he kept in his shoulder holsters and started thinking about how best to enter the house.

Fat, salt-and-pepper hair and with a discoloured, nearly platinum goatee, Pagnan had really bad taste, talked too much and was unbelievably greedy: three traits that allowed him to become the undisputed boss of the Veneto underworld.

Over time, he had been diversifying his activities: loan sharking, arms dealing, armed robberies of security vans, drug trafficking – especially cocaine, distributed by his pushers in all the nightclubs and discos in Veneto. And of course the very remunerative activity of money laundering that had allowed his company, Fresh Air, to become the leading producer of air conditioners in the north-east. And there was a lot to be earned through Fresh Air as well, via crimes such as collusive tendering and of course tax evasion.

As he'd always been able to afford the best lawyers and accountants, he had managed to stay clear of the law courts. Good relations with politicians, both left and right wing, and attendant bribes and backhanders, allowed him to enjoy total immunity. To the money he invested in corruption, he added a healthy entourage of high-end whores passing for escorts, and oceans of cocaine. All of which almost always helped him get what he wanted. And if ultimately somebody wasn't satisfied with that, he always had the right man ready to close their mouth in a committed and professional way.

Until now, everything had been great for Rossano Pagnan. On the job, at least.

His family didn't give him as much satisfaction, though.

His wife and kids were adept at methodically wasting all the money Rossano earned with his hard work. Each of them followed a strictly individual code of conduct, making sure they invested the family's money in a creatively crazy way.

Marisa, his wife, was the kind of woman who infested the supermarkets: fat, buxom and swollen with coke. She complemented this with a fondness for alcohol that caused her to start drinking vodka from the moment she woke up, just to calm her morning nerves. On Sundays she liked to play Rummy with her friends, betting staggering amounts of money that she regularly lost.

Their oldest daughter, Selvaggia, had had the great idea of going to study law in Baton Rouge, Louisiana. Pagnan paid for her studies – several thousand US dollars – and of course a pile extra, such as a Ford Mustang and a Pontiac Firebird. But Selvaggia didn't only like sport cars. She also loved designer clothes: Roberto Cavalli, Vivienne Westwood, Dolce & Gabbana, Jean-Paul Gaultier.

Giacomo, their eight year-old son, spent his time faking various illnesses to skip school and play on his PlayStation, and in his free time he showed his love for their two Rottweilers. Once a week his mother brought him to Media Markt in the Padua Industrial Area, where he bought all the newest electronic devices.

So, Pagnan needed to keep grinding out money not only to satisfy his vast desire for power, but also to be able to keep up with his family's brainless purchases. But he still didn't lose his good spirits; after all, he was happy to be a successful man.

He was wolfing down a portion of thick spaghetti in a Bolognese sauce, his enthusiasm a harbinger of joy. On the table a bottle of Cabernet Franc – half-empty – and a crystal glass – full. Before him an enormous fireplace, no fire lit.

Above the fireplace, a plasma TV screen dominated the room as if it was a Caravaggio. It was showing the local news. But what he saw made him gulp down what he was eating.

"Uh... urgh," he grunted. The enormous mouthful was choking him.

A Filipino waiter in a blue uniform decorated with small crimson mushrooms rushed to him and started vigorously patting his back.

Pagnan spat the cud on his plate just as the pictures of the Galesso twins appeared on the screen. A journalist with a colourless face was explaining how they had met their demise in the toilets of a service station at the hand of a madman who was then beaten within an inch of his life by some heroic girl.

"Wine!" shouted Pagnan, and as he did so he saw Ottorino Longhin's face on the plasma screen. It was all too much, even for a man like him. He started to squirm like a carp that had just bitten a hook.

"Fuckingbastarddirtysonofabitch," he belched as soon as he started to breathe again. Then, staring at the Filipino waiter with his piggy eyes, he started to shout: "Come on, you stupid black ape, what the hell are you looking at? Go call Mule, that genius – everything's going balls up! For fuck's sake!"

The waiter nodded and obeyed.

Mule picked up after ten rings.

"Mule! Where the fuck are you?"

"In Monselice, boss. I'm about to get our money from that asshole Schiavon."

"Leave that shit alone and listen to me!"

"Sure, boss."

"Mule, we are so badly fucked that I can't even start to explain. Imagine a turbine going full speed, splashing shit everywhere. But there's only us there. With our mouths open."

"OK boss, I get the idea."

"Someone killed the twins."

"What twins?"

"Mule, get with the programme, for fuck's sake! The Galesso twins, my insurance policy against jail!"

"Oh shit!"

"Oh, finally! That's the first smart thing you've said!"

Mule clenched his teeth and held his breath. He knew well that in these cases keeping a low profile and behaving like a robot was the best way out.

"But it's not over!"

"Ah!"

"We've been betrayed."

"Fuck."

"Yes! Fuck, fuck, a thousand times fuck! And do you know who by?"

"No."

"Ottorino Longhin, that son of a bitch."

"Shit!"

"Right! Shit! Now, Mule, pay attention, pay close attention to what I'm about to say. The news is reporting that Longhin is at the Padua hospital along with the poor assholes he shot like mockingbirds. Genius! He'll be in a private room, watched by the cops, right?"

"Right, boss."

"So, Mule, what I want you to do, and don't fuck it up, is to go to the hospital and don't leave without him, you got it, Mule? I don't know how you'll do it but I want him, I want him alive, and I want him now. We can't run any risks, and we will if the cops have him. First of all, we need to find out who bought him out. Second, we must make sure he doesn't sell us to the fucking cops. Third, I want to torture him with my own hands. Am I clear, Mule? Take anyone you want, someone like Tripe, Schiavo or what's his face, and bring that son of a bitch to me at the bowling alley. I'll be waiting there. Am I clear?"

"Crystal clear."

"Any questions?"

"Nope."

"I'll see you tonight at the bowling alley, then. Don't fuck this up. See that salary I pay you every month? Today you have to earn it, Mule!" concluded Pagnan, exhausted by the poeticism of his long speech. "The news says it was a bloody mess. Longhin, that twat, lost it and riddled the twins with bullets. We must find out who's behind this, find out and make them pay. Take the guys with you. Understand?"

"Perfectly."

"So one last time: I'll be waiting at the bowling alley."

"Yes boss, I'm going now."

"Yes, right, you better go!"

"One thing, boss."

"What?"

"Well…"

"Come on, Mule, speak! We don't have all day! What's up?"

"Thursday's opening ceremony."

"What the fuck are you talking about?"

"The riding stables!"

"The riding stables?"

"Yes, the riding stables."

"What the fuck is happening, is there an echo? I got it, the riding stables, what about the riding stables? Mule, we're in deep doodoo, you should already be at the hospital and instead you start a game of twenty questions?"

"Boss, I meant… don't forget the opening ceremony for the riding stables. The mayor will be there and you need to deliver the opening speech."

Pagnan felt a mote of revulsion immediately followed by a feeling of dread that clenched his stomach muscles. Right, the riding stables, that spaceship-looking thing the mayor of Muson had built on the Euganean hills. Rossano Pagnan had donated oodles of money to the municipality in order to maintain the appearance of being a really nice man, always the best guarantee of hiding anything illegal.

Pagnan gulped.

"Right," he said, "you're right, Mule. Good that you reminded me of it, but now hang up and go do what you have to."

"OK boss, see you at the bowling alley."

Pagnan was thinking of that goddamned speech. In order to look good he'd prepared a series of quotations good enough to impress a philosopher, but now he couldn't remember any of them. How had he decided to start again? Something like "Horses are extraordinary animals…" but he'd forgotten everything that followed. His mind wandered to the stack of money he'd donated to the mayor and the parish priest, that dirty old sod who shagged his housekeeper and milked shitpiles of money – "offers" he said – off those who'd bought country houses in Muson. Bastards!

Initially it was intended to be a simple riding stable, fences, horses. That was supposed to be it! Then they added a restaurant, a recreation ground, a five-star hotel. What the fuck! How come he had to be their main backer? Still, both out of pride and because it would have probably ended up being a useful move, he'd allowed himself to be screwed over. And now he had to give a fucking speech in front of all those people, restaurant owners, hoteliers, professional people, doctors, lawyers, all people with a lot of money who liked that corner of the hills, who considered it a safe harbour to rest after a long week's work.

To him personally, that stupid idea of building a riding stable up in the hills was trouble from day one. Like that time when, driving home, he destroyed his car after hitting a boar. A furious, hairy beast that some asshole had decided to repopulate the hills with, pretty much handing over one of the nicest areas in Veneto to a bunch of wild pigs that in a few years had bred at a ridiculous rate. Which was one more thing he couldn't understand: they were boars, not rabbits! Still... still he had hit one, and anyway it was Monday, only three days to go, and he couldn't remember a single passage of the speech he was supposed to give.

# 3

Thanks to Rossano Pagnan's contacts with some of the doctors in the Padua hospital, Mule knew exactly where he'd find Longhin: Geriatric Medicine, room number six, a single room guarded night and day by two agents of the Penitentiary Police.

Useful information, but by no means a solution. He needed to find a way to sneak into the hospital, keep the policemen at bay, get to the ground floor with Longhin, get out and leave: nearly impossible. Not to mention all the hassle the hospital workers and the patients might create.

Dress up as a doctor, sneak into Longhin's

room in a white coat and leave with the patient after a while? Only in a movie.

Still, the guys expected him to take charge. He was the highest ranking and nobody would even think of disobeying his orders. The negative side of being called Mule and being Pagnan's right hand man was that he had to take responsibility for complex operations like this one. Even though he always made up a thousand reasons to be suspicious, Pagnan, that fucking lardass, trusted his mule after all.

He had earned that nickname in the field, so to speak. He never gave up; maybe he was slower or less smart than his adversaries, but he was always able to stand up again and wait for the moment his enemy made a mistake. He waited for his opponent to lower his guard and then kicked out, and made sure the job was done. Properly.

And not only that: he'd also proved he was completely loyal to the gang. He'd been inside for twelve years for armed robbery and as an accessory to first degree murder. His loyalty continued throughout his forced sojourn at the Due Palazzi prison in Padua. There he was always on his best behaviour, going so far as to join the team of inmates that produced the best Easter cakes in town. Pagnan was grateful: he had showered him in money and picked him as his right-hand man.

But now the issue with Longhin needed to be resolved. He'd been trying to think of a solution less dangerous than the first one that popped into his head, but no luck so far. So he decided to focus the operation on the three key actions of a brave but desperate gangster.

Enter the hospital with guns drawn, take hostages and threaten bloodshed.

That's what Saverio Donolato, aka Mule, was thinking as he drove closer to the entrance of the hospital, in Via Giustiniani 2.

He cleared his throat, nervously fiddled with his gel-tamed hair, then checked in the rearview mirror to see how the blue double-breasted coat he'd bought some days earlier fit him. He loosened his regimental-style tie a little and adjusted the collar of his long woollen coat.

Then he gave some minimal instructions to the guys.

"Right, Tripe, here we are. You stay here, arse planted on the driver's seat. As soon as you see us coming back, gun the engine and take off at light speed. That's not hard, is it?"

"Consider it done," replied Tripe nodding with his fierce smile. His handlebar moustache highlighted his smug expression, his grey eyes shining like stones in a riverbed.

"Schiavo, Polenta, the pair of you with me."

"OK Mule," replied Schiavo checking behind his back to make sure his nickel .357 Magnum was nicely tucked in his trousers and hidden by the jacket of the perfect grey suit he had picked for the occasion.

"No problem," said Polenta.

"Good, so... let's go."

They got out of the cobalt blue Audi A3 and started walking up the silver ramp to the main hospital reception, like three scarecrows dressed up for some big event.

As soon as they got to the hall, the smell of disinfectant and mashed potatoes assaulted their nostrils. They carried on, staying cool, and climbed to the first floor, taking the stairs rather than the lift.

Three hardened killers, tense and ready to dance, their dream of an easy hit about to shatter like glass. Which they were just about to step all over. They covered their faces with balaclavas and opened the door leading to Geriatric Medicine.

They were in.

"Rock 'n' roll!" shouted Polenta, and drew a shining Colt .45 from his shoulder holster, placing it right between the eyes of the head nurse, a big woman with hair as orange as an egg yolk, frozen behind her desk.

"If you so much as flinch, I'll make jam of your fucking brain," he added.

"No bullshit, you pair!" Schiavo kept his .357 trained on the two policemen guarding Longhin's room, ready to shoot.

"Quick, bitch!" roared Mule towards a small, pretty nurse. "Find me a fucking wheelchair or you're done thinking for good. Now!" As he spoke, he extracted his Glock .17 from his shoulder holster and screwed on a silencer.

The girl hesitated. For too long.

Mule pulled the trigger.

Shot.

Hit.

Scream.

Spurt of blood on the floor.

The nurse, her arm seriously hurt.

Mule knew he'd gone too far but he couldn't show it. What the fuck was he doing? Had detention made him go crazy? He needed to appear to be in control. Because Polenta couldn't wait to tear the whole wing to pieces. That's how he was. And Mule was sending the wrong message.

"What the fuck are you doing?" shouted one

of the policemen as he instinctively went for his gun.

"Hey, mate. Touch your iron and this becomes a slaughterhouse."

As he spat the words through clenched teeth, Mule stood in front of the nurse he'd shot and drilled a hole through her head with a stare.

She got it straight away and pointed at one of the rooms. Mule went there after having looked Polenta in the eye to make sure he understood that it had only been a warning shot. He didn't want the kids painting the walls their favourite colour while he was away.

Thankfully, Polenta nodded.

A few seconds later Mule returned, pushing a wheelchair that looked well past its prime.

"Right," he said. "Nobody leave the room or I'll fucking kill the lot of you! I'll turn you into mincemeat seasoned with lead! Understand, you old farts?" Then he spat towards a couple of white heads that had dared peek into the corridor, "Do you understand? If I find out you've rung a bell, a rattle or any other shit, if a guard or some fucking consultant comes I'll tear you all to pieces. Yeah? Am I clear enough?"

After that volley of threats, a surreal silence fell. It was hard to believe how much he'd just talked, and he was far from being a public speaker. But he felt that by barking insults he had entranced his audience, and more importantly, he had regained the pizzazz of his best years. His assistants stared at him as if in love. The policemen were frozen. Two Egyptian sphinxes. He was pleased.

Before the effect of his tirade died out, he rushed into Longhin's room. He found him in bed, covered in bandages and plasters, swollen eyes open wide. In his sarcophagus, Tutan-khamen probably wore less bandages than this bastard, Mule thought to himself.

"Hi, you son of a bitch. We're going for a spin."

Longhin didn't reply. He had already visualised the whole movie of what awaited him, including a gigantic, bright red "The End".

"Bet you can't walk, can you?"

With the calmness and stoicism of a dying man, Longhin moved his ass from the bed to the wheelchair without making a sound.

"Well done, asshole. You better not bust my balls, right?"

Tutankhamen nodded.

"Damn it, Otto, cat got your tongue? But it's OK. It's OK, better like this."

Outside the room it looked like they were playing a game of statues: everything was frozen, exactly like it was a minute ago.

Polenta was holding the fat head nurse and the bleeding girl at gunpoint, Schiavo the two policemen.

No noise. Everybody showing an impressive maturity.

"Hey, they behaved," said Schiavo.

"Hi Longhin. You know what's coming, eh?" and with an evil grin, left hand held like a knife, Polenta mimed slitting someone's throat.

"Let's head!" Mule said interrupting him. "I'll go to the lift and put this asshole in it. Soon as I'm in, the two of you follow me with a nurse each. If we don't fuck up we'll be out in no time.

"Ah!" he added, louder. "To those who are here and those who aren't. If you think of calling someone or playing the hero," and he looked at the two policemen, "the two women will be the first to go to Heaven. Understood?"

The silence of deep space.

"Now unfasten your holsters. What, you think I'm stupid?"

The cops looked at each other, then did what they were told.

"That's it. Nice and slow. Now put your hands up."

They did and Schiavo removed their weapons.

"Very good. Thank you all for your cooperation. And goodbye, it's been a pleasure."

Mule started walking towards the lift, pushing the wheelchair in which a trembling Longhin was sitting. Schiavo and Polenta caught up with him just in time, one arm around the nurses' necks, guns to their heads.

In ten seconds they got to the ground floor.

The door slid open.

In front of them, two white-gowned doctors with plastic cups of coffee were walking up the corridor in a self-important sort of way.

"You better not say a word, you two!" barked Mule from under his balaclava.

The doctors goggled at the parade of hostages and guns leaving the lift.

One of them dropped his cup.

"Maaah…" he groaned.

"What are you doing?" said the other. And, with a slightly too cheeky tone, he added: "I'll call the police!"

"You really don't fucking get it!" barked Mule. He lunged forward and hit the doc's chin with a right hook, immediately followed by a jab. The doctor flew backwards, landed spitting blood and a front tooth that left a dark gap in his mouth.

Mule rubbed his knuckles, snorted and cleared his throat to stop the burning feeling that had started bothering him.

But it didn't go away.

And his troubles were far from over.

The hospital was turning out to be a real treasure house of obstacles. To put it nicely. And his patience was running really low.

From the opposite end of the corridor, a nurse in a mint green uniform, who had watched the whole scene unfurl, screamed as if someone had just extracted her kidneys.

Mule took charge of the situation. His way. He was sick and tired of all the fucking tension.

"This is it!" he hollered. "I've been shouting for the last ten minutes asking you all to stop pissing me off!"

He was really worn out. He started waving his Glock 17.

"The two of you go ahead, and make sure they can see the women," he ordered Schiavo and Polenta. His voice had lowered suddenly.

They walked on, hiding behind the head nurse and the wounded girl. Mule followed them with his priceless charge.

The doctors from the elevator were still staring at them, slightly bewildered.

As soon as the six of them turned the corner into the main hall the shouting started multiplying. A scene worthy of Dante's *Inferno*: a couple of old geezers started running away with their IVs dangling from their stands; a bunch of

MATTEO STRUKUL                73

paramedics burst out from behind the reception desk and vanished in under a second; a Moroccan with a bloody arm started shouting like a man possessed.

Mule turned his gaze towards his men.

"Let's keep our cool," he said. "We're professionals and we'll get out of here unharmed."

But it was a hairy situation. The police would arrive very soon. The plan – if indeed there had ever been one – had gone completely tits up.

And the worst was yet to come.


A security guard appeared from one of the doors on the hall and charged at Schiavo, head down, while the head nurse bit his arm and forced him to let go.

It all happened in a split second.

A thin blade shone in the security guard's hand.

Mule shouted, but to no avail.

The scalpel dragged lethally across Schiavo's neck, which started spurting blood like a fountain.

Polenta screamed. The sudden assault on his friend's life had managed to destroy his self-control.

He pushed the young nurse away and started shooting with his Colt .45.

He shot all around him, towards the fleeing head nurse and Schiavo's killer who in the meantime had stood up and was holding a P38 Special, ready to fire.

Two hollow point bullets found their way to the back of the head nurse, who crashed to the floor. Three hit the head of the security guard, who turned into a small red volcano belching out blood and brains.

Polenta grabbed the nurse with the bleeding arm by the hair. She had remained there, kneeling, crying in silence. He pulled her up.

"Move, bitch! Or do you want to die as well?"

They started running.

Mule was pushing the wheelchair with the mummified Longhin in it. Polenta followed, dragging the nurse behind him like a lifeless corpse.

They opened the screen doors to the cold, pungent evening air.

They kept running.

Long seconds later, they heard screams booming in their ears. But they were safe, one step from the car.

Just time to lift Longhin up and throw him into the back seat. Then Mule and Polenta got in.

"Where's Schiavo?" asked the waiting Tripe.

"Dead!" replied Mule.

And with that, the cobalt blue Audi A3 accelerated away as if an invisible monster had bitten its ass.

# 4

"I think she's at home. Alone," said Zhang Wen.

"You think? You mean you're not sure?" replied Xan Jingyu.

"Just about... but I saw her in action, she's really fast. So try not to underestimate her."

"We won't," said Wu Jingjing tidying up his sleek, silky hair.

"There's a low wall around the house. We climb over it, run through the garden and then split up. I go in through the living room, you go through the kitchen."

"Are the doors open?"

"Yes. While I was waiting for you I took a walk around. Both French windows are open." .

"She's not waiting for us, is she?" asked Xan, a hint of suspicion in his shrill voice.

"No chance."

"Are you sure she didn't notice you following her?" insisted Wu. He knew Zhang and didn't trust him completely, since he was the spoiled nephew of the biggest fish in the Talking Daggers gang.

Spoiled and completely mental. There was a legend in the clan: that he had a cellar containing only a butcher's table and a freezer. On the occasions he tortured his victims before he killed them, he liked to keep something as a souvenir: a hand, a foot, the head. He stored his trophies in the freezer, a kind of macabre frozen archive.

Probably all bullshit. But there's some truth behind every rumour. That's what Wu was thinking when Zhang said, "Hey, guys, what can I tell you? I've been very careful. Now, listen up: I'll enter first through the living room, then the two of you through the kitchen. We'll flank her. She can't be in two places at the same time."

The last part of his speech sounded just like a Kongzi saying to the two men. So, free of all doubts, Zhang, Xan and Wu sprang into action.

Zhang climbed the low wall and approached the French window that opened onto the garden. Meanwhile Xan and Wu did the same on the other side of the house, where the kitchen was located.

From inside, they could hear the sound of running water, a shower, almost certainly. The red dreadlocked girl was going through her rinse cycle, so sure she'd not been followed that she ignored even the most basic safety measures.

Zhang thought of that scene in *Psycho*, when Norman Bates stabs Marion Crane in the shower. Although Zhang had two Walther PPK 7.65s and was ready to make a ghost of the woman by riddling her with bullets, shame they needed her alive to find out where the money was.

He crossed the garden, nimble and sure-footed like a wild cat, smelling the earth and noticing the purple leaves of the radicchio. Past the vegetable garden and the shed, he was already enjoying the success of the raid he considered was being conducted in textbook fashion.

He paused at the small marble patio in front of the living room window. He raised the silenced gun with two hands, pointing it straight ahead, ready to shoot at the first sign of trouble.

He knew he had to be careful: he'd seen what that girl could do. And it was enough for him. She couldn't be underestimated, he kept telling himself. But everything seemed to be under control. He focussed on the French window.

He was so focussed that he hardly realised as he entered that something really sharp and really cold had whipped at his wrists.

"Aah!"

What had struck his hands?

Only then he noticed that the living room floor was covered with a huge plastic sheet.

No!

Zhang stood frozen in terror, a scream choking in his throat. His legs gave way to inertia and to a feeling of dismay that permeated his whole body like a weak but continuous electric current.

Where the hell was his gun?

No! Where the hell were his hands?

A katana!

The Japanese sword shone in the fists of the girl with the red dreadlocks.

She was standing next to him, smiling, staring at him through strange glasses with shiny yellow lenses. She had appeared from nowhere with the speed of a silent Fury.

Zhang couldn't believe it! His hands were on the floor with the gun.

He would have liked to scream in pain until his vocal cords tore, but he didn't have the time to make a single sound: the girl pivoted on her left leg, traced a perfect arc in the air and hit his face with surgical precision.

Zhang felt the blow. His body crumpled, fell with a dull thud and rolled on the plastic sheet covering the living room floor.

A dull thud.

Xan and Wu had felt it too, while they moved, fast and careful, in the kitchen.

But after the thud they heard nothing else.

They looked at each other in silence. Then Xan, holding his trusted Beretta calibre .9 tightly, entered the corridor followed by Wu, a couple of yards behind him.

As soon as he reached the living room door, Xan saw something he really didn't want to see: a new, bloodcurdling version of Zhang.

A instant later, Xan saw the girl, covered in a black latex suit and wearing glasses with yellow lenses.

Grasping the situation, aiming and firing took place in one instinctive flow. But he missed.

That bloody redhead moved like a cat. As the shot was fired she jumped to one side, pressed with her hands and legs on the wall and somersaulted over Xan's head like a circus acrobat.

Mila landed behind him and swiped his legs from under him with a low kick. The Chinaman went down, powerless, and when he was close enough to kiss the floor, Mila unsheathed her katana and sliced upwards, left to right.

Xan's head, perfectly separated from the rest of his body, flew through the air in a series of purple, grim rotations and ended up next to Zhang, who was nearly drowned in the blood that was still flowing from his severed wrists.

A second *thud*.

Preceded by a shot muffled by the silencer.


Wu was frozen.

That girl was awesome, a real professional killer. She had planned every detail: she had deceived them; she had waited for them; she was killing them one after the other. And they had completely missed the whole set up. They'd walked into her house like flies into a spider's web. A black widow.

Wu couldn't think; thick, salty beads of perspiration on his forehead. He noticed four video cameras in the four corners of the room, clearly closed-circuit.

Why the hell were those there?

What the hell was he doing here anyway, in what looked like a movie set but with real blood instead of tomato juice?

He was here to kill a redhead who knew how to hold her own in a fight and he needed to be watchful of her.

His eyes focussed again on Mila.

The girl was staring at him with an amused and somehow pitying expression.

"Forget it," she said.

She is gorgeous, thought Wu. But she is also too quick, strong, unpredictable.

He was never going to make it.

He tried anyway.

Raised his HK P7.

Shot.

The bullet hit the wall: Mila had taken to the air like the Angel of Death and, face to face with Wu, hit him really hard in the stomach.

Wu understood that it was over, and he had not started yet. A single punch like that one shouldn't have been hurting so bad. But it had taken his breath away and now he was on all fours, his face only inches from the floor.

With the heel of her boot Mila crushed the hand holding the gun then kicked the weapon away. Then she stepped on his other hand, crushing it as well. Finally she unsheathed her katana and slashed at him from above.

Wu's head left his body at an impossible angle, then hit the floor.

Wu's corpse fell down with a dull thud. Three.

Mila watched the blood gush from the beheaded body.

Luckily she had thought of the plastic sheet.

She took her specs off and made sure that the minicams in the frame had recorded the three scenes.

She opened the glass door of the drinks cupboard. Pressed the "stop" button and ejected the disc from the console which controlled the closed-circuit cameras around the house.

Very good. She even had some panning shots.

She needed to cauterize Zhang's wounds as soon as possible to make sure he didn't die of blood loss. If he died, all that evening's work would be for nothing.

She lifted the unconscious young man's body and dragged it to the kitchen. Then she turned on the cooker, the biggest flame burning as high as possible.

Zhang was starting to recover. But when he opened his eyes he could see only the girl and the blue-orange flame.

Mila didn't waste any time. She sealed his mouth with a large square of duct tape, grabbed his arms and placed them in the flame.

Zhang tried to scream, but his voice bounced off the duct tape and fell back into his throat.

"Don't move," she said, "or you'll bleed to death."

The smell of burned flesh thickened the air in

the kitchen. Mila struggled to avoid retching.

When it was done, she applied a snow-white bandage on the stumps. Then she tightened two leather laces under his armpits and over his shoulders: his arms would be dead flesh by now anyway, but trussed up like this he would survive for the moment – as long as she needed him to.

"Stand up and walk. To the bedroom."

Zhang stared at her, silent, completely motionless.

"Lie down on the bed and spread your legs."

Mila bound his right leg with duct tape to the bar at the bottom of the bed. Then did the same to his left. Then she repeated the drill with his arms or what was left of them, fastening them to the headboard. Then she went to the garden and took a burlap sack from the shed.

She went back to the living room.

She grabbed the heads of the other two Chinamen by the hair and dumped them in the sack, then wrapped the bodies in the plastic sheet.

Now she needed to bury them in the garden. She could wait for darkness as an extra precaution. But her house was pretty isolated and the other half of the semi-detached was empty. And caution didn't come easily.

She dragged the corpses of the two Chinamen to the shed and left them on the floor.

She went back inside. Carefully folded the plastic sheet and put it in a big, black bin liner.

Then she changed her clothes. She put on discoloured jeans, brown boots and a grey Nike tank top.

She went back to the shed, took out a pickaxe and a shovel and started to dig a deep, wide hole to bury the two corpses.

# 5

*From Mila Zago's journal:*

Dear Dr Chiara Berton,
 My name is Mila Zago and I am exactly
what you will find out I am.
 A killer.
 Before I start I'd like to tell you that I
would have liked to be different, but this is
how it turned out. I'm not looking for
excuses, I don't need any. Anyway, I
wouldn't go back.
 I never met my mother. She left my
father only a few days after I was born.
 Why?

Because he was a police officer and had a hellish life and I was a mistake – they hadn't planned me. She was very young; she didn't have the heart to arrange an abortion but she didn't feel strong enough to stay with us and bring me up either.

This is how I explained her walking out to myself; I never found a better explanation. I have never been a religious woman.

My father was almost never home. Like all the people in his business he spent the whole day, every day, working – police headquarters, reports, investigations, courts of justice. Sound familiar?

I spent my childhood with my father's parents, who educated me with a little discipline. Nine months every year we lived in the countryside – Reschigliano, a hamlet just outside Campodarsego. I'd go to school in the morning and spend my afternoons doing sports. We spent the summer in Enego, in the Seven Communities plateau, where grandpa owned a house.

During the spring, especially on Saturdays or Sundays, if my dad managed to get off work, I'd bike-ride with him on the Brenta embankments. We'd bring a tartan rug, a bag with some chicken salad in a plastic box and the cookies grandma baked, and we'd just sit there watching the river rocking in its bed. Those were days without a care that lasted until the sun went down, at which point I'd climb onto the crossbar of my dad's bicycle; on the way back I'd hear dad's breathing get heavier when we climbed the short slopes. During autumn we'd take long, leisurely walks on the paths that separated the fields or the vines. On those occasions I'd smell the tobacco that permeated his clothes all the time.

A simple, well organised life. Characterised by a strong sense of duty. Grandpa was a retired army general. He loved me, but he was unwavering when it came to teaching me to respect the rules and take care of my fitness. He was very important in moulding my character and body. After swimming in the early years came athletics, running, the gym.

During the summer, in the mountains of Enego, I'd run over long stretches of pasture, faster and faster every day. "You need to gain stamina," he kept telling me.

And then the "fitness trails" and the floor exercises. Every day I'd do endless repetitions of sit-ups and push-ups.

Year after year, I kept improving my stamina; my legs were coils ready to spring into action. All this constant, intense training happened under the gaze of grandpa's watchful grey eyes. I never complained. I was happy to do what he told me. I didn't want to disappoint him, I suppose. I spoke little and worked hard: it had been clear to me since day one that if I wanted to do something with my life I had to count solely on my determination.

My hands, arms, legs, became perfectly tuned instruments.

A few years later they would become weapons.

And then? And then there was grandma.

She was in charge of my domestic education. The roles of husband and wife were clearly defined in my grandparents' life; maybe that's why I never had any rebellious notions.

With her I'd make gnocchi. I'd roll out the dough then I'd knead it until it became like a long snake. When I started cutting it I'd watch it lose its tail, one piece at the time, on the flour-covered table. And then I'd nick the soft little balls with a fork. It was fun.

I would also bake lasagne and sauté edible boletus. Being in the kitchen was beautiful. I'd discover a completely different world and listen to stories my gran would tell me in her sweet voice.

I loved nature too, and I liked going to look for mushrooms in the woods. I'd leave with grandpa on his K70 while the sun was coming out and, through hairpin bends and back roads, we'd go high up on the fringes of Mount Lisser or near Marcesina or Campomulo. Wild, mysterious names that tickled my young girl's curiosity.

"Check under the pines, not under the larches!" It was like a mantra. Grandpa would keep repeating it until he was blue in the face. Although I also found good mushrooms between stones and in the grass.

Thus the years went by: in a golden cage made of rules transmitted with love.

Until then everything was great. A simple girl with her little adventures, growing up healthy thanks to clean air and exercise.

Then, one day, the shit hit the fan.

The endless, constant training became a crazy rush towards revenge, a revenge that sooner or later would destroy those who were guilty.

And they had a name.

Pagnan.

My father was killed during a robbery in a restaurant.

Killed like a dog.

You probably heard the story. It's been talked about quite a bit.

The person behind the robbery and the slaughter that followed was Rossano Pagnan: the papers wrote about it, the TV news hinted at it. Everybody knew. But the justice machine you belong to yourself returned a not guilty verdict due to lack of evidence.

And that was the least of it. So to speak.

That day I was there as well. We had gone to the races. My dad didn't bet often, only occasionally, for fun. He had a certain instinct for picking the right horse. After the races we would go to eat in a nice restaurant. Da Renzo, it was called. It's not there any longer. After that episode, it had to close. For good.

Dad loved that place. We went at least twice a month. It was a ritual he wanted to maintain, even though his salary was pretty low.

From what I gathered, there was some loan-sharking going on and one day Pagnan decided to send some of his men to make the owner understand that it's always better to pay your debts.

He also knew that his men would find my father there. My father was investigating him and had probably been breathing down his neck. It's fairly certain that Pagnan had had the place cased and thought he could kill two birds with one stone.

It's more than ten years ago, and I can't remember everything clearly. I only know that at a certain point I found myself staring at my father; he was on the floor, gasping, blowing bubbles of blood and I was looking down at him, frozen to my seat. I wanted to help him but I couldn't move a muscle. I was scared. Really scared. Pagnan's men were screaming like devils, all wearing black balaclavas on their heads.

They lifted me out of my chair and put a huge gun in my mouth. One of them held

my face in one of his big, rough hands. My
jaw hurt.

They carried me out of the restaurant. At
the door I managed to turn around and
saw my father crawling on his belly,
stretching his arms towards me. He
couldn't speak; he was gurgling, his spit
red, and he was trailing blood. I was
crying. I couldn't do anything else. That
day, I cried all my tears. All those I had
been granted, a lifetime's worth.

There were four men, all big and
wearing black.

They threw me in a car. The one at the
wheel drove like a man possessed. The two
in the back seat crunched mint candies.
The one in the passenger seat had shiny,
gelled, black hair. Smelled like lavender.
His hair, I mean.

I was dog-tired. I was terrified. Nobody
was talking. There was a kind of silence
that I'm not able to describe, it seemed to
me to anticipate something shocking. I
think I learned from them to be quiet. I
understood that speaking is pointless if
you're planning to hurt someone. I was
afloat in that silence, but I was aware that
sooner or later I would be drowning in a

sea of pain.

At a certain point the silence was broken by a question that made my skin crawl.

"Saverio, where are we going to fuck this one?" asked one of the two men flanking me.

"Hey, you really are a twat," replied the guy with the hair gel. "How many times do I need to tell you not to use my fucking name?" And silence fell again in the car, sharp as ice.

I still have those words etched in my memory. I'll never be able to erase them, not even in the afterlife.

We left town. Someone – I can't remember who – said that he needed to warm up. The man with the hair gel motioned the driver to stop. They left the car and pushed me into the middle of a field. I stumbled and fell.

I remained face down, staring at the hard, cold ground scratching my knees.

They raped me, the four of them, one after another.

I felt the warm breath of the two men who had been in the back seat on my neck. It smelled of mint.

Then it was the turn of the driver.

The man with the gelled hair was last.
He held my neck tight in his hands,
whispering insults in my ears: I was just a
bitch in heat, a cocksucking slut who liked
a good fucking. My head was spinning like
a merry-go-round gone haywire.

They all came, one after another.

When they were done I remained bent
forward, mud on my face.

They left me there, between the rubble
and the clods of earth of a ploughed field.

Abandoned like a bag of trash.

I can't remember how long I remained
on my knees. It felt like forever. Then I
stood up again. My legs were trembling. It
felt like my stomach was trying to scream. I
put my jeans back on. My thighs were
covered in scratches.

Somehow I made it back to the road and
started walking along it like a robot,
pretending I didn't feel the burning
sensation between my legs. I walked a long
while.

Then I saw, far ahead, the red and blue
Esso sign. I got there. I couldn't bear it any
longer. I got to the toilets behind the bar.
Luckily they were empty. I hugged the sink
and threw up everything I'd eaten.

Spaghetti, meatballs, potatoes. My mouth
and chin were covered in a mixture of spit,
tears and regurgitated food. A dull roar
struggled to escape my lips, my way of
venting the rage that had started to invade
me like a giant wave.

After having soaked and balled up a
bunch of paper towels, I went into one of
the stalls. I lowered my jeans, being very
careful not to touch the filthy bowl with
my bleeding thighs, and slowly wiped
between my legs with the wet paper.

Before going back out into the open I
washed my hands and face once more.
Then I looked at myself in the mirror.

It was better now. My face was swollen,
my hair wet and sticking to my face. I
looked a little worse for wear, nothing
more.

I went into the bar and asked for a cup
of tea. Then I called grandpa from the
public phone.

That day, I changed forever.

I never told anyone what happened.
Maybe I already knew I would never be
able to go back. I can't explain – it was as if
something had broken inside me. I felt
drained. I don't know if you ever felt

anything like that. It feels a lot like being torn apart, a deep slash, so deep it scars your soul.

A strange instinct took hold, slowly.

A predator's instinct.

I didn't talk for a whole year. I communicated with my grandparents using just my eyes. They respected my grief.

I realised I wasn't strong enough. I intensified my training. My sessions in the gym became endless. I started training in martial arts and practiced on shooting ranges.

Revenge became my religion. I had cut off all human contact, lost the power of speech, given up on my dreams. One after another. The meaning I looked for in life had been torn apart. By the guilty laziness of a cowardly judge, by men's bloody, animal greed.

They would come to me on their knees, begging for mercy.

One day I'd strike them with a force that would make them shatter.

Them and those like them.

Parasites.

Criminals.

Roaches who left their holes to patter about on the corpses of their victims.

I promised myself I'd kill them all, kick them all down.

Like bowling pins.

# 6

The pins.

There were no pins.

In their place, Ottorino Longhin. His mouth held shut with wire that went between his teeth and locked his jaws in a thin clasp.

He was leaning backwards slightly, knees apart, his hands tied behind his back and his feet bound together under his buttocks by a wad of duct tape. Tears streamed down his face. He was wearing only jeans and a tank top. His face was covered in bruises and white plaster that made him look like a gothic version of Harlequin. A thick rope tied him by the neck to a beam a foot or so behind him that ensured he couldn't move without choking himself.

He was at the far end of a bowling lane, shining in the honey hue of its wood, smooth as a billiard table.

At the opposite end of the lane, Rossano Pagnan stared at him, smiling. His white linen shirt was open on his chest like the threadbare curtains in an old theatre. Revealing tufts of grey hair and the gold of a thick chain around his bull-like neck. Linen trousers with a skull motif in a pirate theme, and bright pink Crocs on his feet. A regular feature of Veneto fashion.

Around him a crowd of minions enjoying the show. The heating was cranked up and the temperature was semi-tropical, so much so that Hell would have felt like a Canadian ice hockey rink in comparison.

The massive bowling alley was revolving in Longhin's protruding eyes. Thirty-two lanes: white, red and blue; at the entrance, a bar as big as an aircraft carrier, small tables everywhere, looking just like a typical American diner. The sweet smell of the caramel popcorn made the area around him an oasis of even warmer air, whipped by gusts of an appalling stench. Around the popcorn, glasses of some kind of spritz, the regular local aperitif, with Aperol. Orange, like traffic lights in a glass.

"I need to tell the assholes in maintenance to

open some windows here," said Pagnan wiping his lips with the white sleeve of his shirt. "So, you piece of shit, are you going to talk?" he added looking at Longhin.

Who could only shake his head.

"Otto, you're a real dickhead. Don't you get it? If you remain silent, we'll tear you to pieces. If you talk, you might stand a chance."

"Ugh," said Longhin. A grunt of pain rather than an answer.

"Look, if you're afraid the assholes you betrayed me to are going to do something to you, well…" carried on Pagnan raising a grey eyebrow like a fat old wolf, "I'll make mincemeat out of you. Do you understand, you piece of shit, you traitor, you Judas?"

Pagnan kept talking like a politician giving a speech, as he always did when he had the whip hand.

And on this occasion he definitely did.

First of all, the building lay in the middle of the Veneto farmland like a monolith on the face of the moon. Second: it belonged to him. Third: it was closed on Mondays and Tuesdays.

So there was nowhere safer to torture a back-stabbing traitor in the whole of Veneto. As luck would have it, Longhin had had the brilliant idea of getting caught on a Monday.

Pagnan was beaming. He had decided he'd work the bastard slowly. Like in the old days, when he'd have camped out here until he'd ripped the bastard's eternal soul from his body. So to speak.

Mule was enjoying the show, staring at Longhin at the end on the lane. He took a spritz from the table, swallowed a couple of mouthfuls then said, "Because of this asshole, poor old Schiavo lost his life. Now I want to have some fun." With a glittering smirk he took a shiny, deep blue bowling ball. He raised it to his chest and caressed it with his other hand. "Here it comes, Otto!" he shouted.

With a short run up and a nice power stroke, Mule rolled the ball along the lane. It was a precise shot, straight and quite hard.

Longhin's eyes opened wide. The ball was rolling towards him, getting faster and faster.

It hit him in the crotch. He shouted and pulled against the noose around his throat.

"Strike!" shouted Mule. He gulped down the rest of his spritz, wiped his lips with a paper towel and started doing the twist at his end of the lane.

Pagnan exploded in wild laughter, and so did his gang. Then he stood up and chose a ball for himself.

He jumped to the foul line, moving his thick

legs as fast as he could, his belly swinging; his bright pink Crocs helped make him look like a hippo doing a psychedelic dance number. The ball left his hand in a swing that ate up the ground at speed, only stopping when it came into contact with Longhin's right kneecap.

*Crack!*

"Mmpf." A whimper of pain.

"Come on, Otto. Talk and all this shit will be over," Pagnan encouraged him, and started walking down the bowling lane towards his prisoner.

When he was halfway there, his mobile rang. He checked the display and took a long breath. His eyes filled with dread. Resigned, he clicked the keypad and took the call.

"Hey, you old scoundrel, how's things?" Benny Marcato's voice was low and smooth. The Mayor of Muson always talked as if he was speaking on the radio.

Pagnan grinned and cleared his throat, gathering all his diplomacy skills.

"Hey, my dear sir, how are you?"

"Besides the fact that it's only two days to the great event, everything's fine. I can't complain." A pause. "Of course, it's going to be a great event, right?"

Pagnan rolled his eyes. That stuff was wearing

him out. Riding stables and horses, horses and riding stables. He was busy demolishing a man with a bowling ball and this asshole was spoiling what ought to be a sacred pleasure. Sometimes life is merciless. "Yes, it'll be the crowning moment of the magnificent work we've done together," he managed to say.

"I was thinking the same, you know. Even that old idiot of a parish priest is beaming his face off. Have you decided on the key points of your speech yet?"

"Well, I have a lot on my mind…"

What the hell was he talking about? He remembered fuck all. His memory was a black hole and improvising on the topic of horses was going to be about as easy as roping a ferret.

"Wonderful. And remember the children, say something about the children."

"Of course."

"We need to make the audience feel comfortable. Or rather, make all the cash cows happy to be joining a super-exclusive club."

"Sure thing."

"We need to reassure them that their children will be treated like little princes and princesses. Not only will the little dears learn how to ride a horse, but they'll be constantly monitored for their protection. There'll be no chance of them getting hurt. Anyway, a horse is a child's best friend."

Benny Marcato was completely out of his mind. What was he thinking? Was he expecting him, Rossano Pagnan, to behave like a circus seal? Yes, of course, a gloss of respectability was important, but not so much to allow that fuckwit to brainwash him. He decided to end the call.

"That's great, Benny, thanks for ringing. Now I really have to go."

"Of course, Rossano. Sorry for calling you so late, I just wanted to check everything was going according to plan."

"Don't worry. The opening speech is in safe hands."

"That's great. I count on it, my good man!"

"Don't worry."

"OK, have a nice evening."

"Same to you."

Pagnan's head filled with malevolent thoughts but he sent them scurrying away as if they were sewer rats. He breathed through his nose.

"So," he said, trying to preserve some dignity, "where were we? Ah, yes, I was coming to you, matey." He recommenced his walk towards the end of the bowling lane.

The other members of the gang were looking at him, expectantly. The Mayor's call had not been long enough to make everyone lose the quiet lust for blood that had inhabited them since the start of the evening. Each had used the enforced break their own way. Mule had made himself his umpteenth spritz: icy cold sparkling wine straight from the cooler, Aperol, very fizzy water and lots of ice. He could have drunk twenty of them on the go. Spritz was a real drug for him, and even though people said that only poofs used Aperol and he should use Campari, well, he didn't give a shit. Because he was Mule, nobody could piss him off, and also – after the Big White Chief – he was the one they all had to deal with, like it or not.

Not far away from Mule, Tripe, at a small table, was having a taste of his favourite meal, the rich, sour smell of it filling his nostrils. In front of his eyes was a huge bowl of Veneto-style tripe. While chewing his fingernails waiting for the others to come back from their hospital raid with the traitor-mummy, he'd grown hungry. He had a mountain of nosh prepared by Pretty Boy, the bowling alley cook, a confirmed womanizer and former butcher, who knew every cut of meat inside out, and was a custodian of traditional cuisine.

Pretty Boy had left the kitchen and started sharpening a battery of knives he had carefully set up on a wooden table next to the bowling lanes.

He was wearing a blue apron like some cowherd from South Tirol. It was stained with blood and worn over a white undershirt, combat trousers and hiking boots. His huge chest expanded under a head covered in a mane of thick, jet-black hair. Ice cold eyes and a pretty big nose contributed to his determined, resolute appearance.

Pagnan was standing in front of Longhin. He looked in his eyes then slapped him twice, the sound like a whiplash.

"Dirty scab. Decided not to speak, eh?"

"Aargh," was the answer.

Pagnan started tightening the wire mask that locked Longhin's jaws together.

Tighter and tighter.

"Does that hurt, asshole?"

Tighter and tighter.

"Uugh."

Tighter.

Blood started to flow copiously from Longhin's cracked lips. In a pointless attempt to free himself from the grip, he was flailing about like a rabid dog on a chain.

"Boss, he'll never be able to talk like that," Polenta pointed out.

"I don't believe I asked your opinion, shit for brains," he replied. "Actually, while you're in the mood for shit, go tell Pretty Boy to come over with a couple of carving knives. Let's see how ballsy our cowboy is."

"Coming, Boss," said Pretty Boy immediately, as if he'd been called to go collect a million euro lottery win.

"No, wait," Pagnan said. "I want that pain in the ass, Polenta, to ask you."

Mule chuckled.

Tripe froze, a forkful of food halfway between the plate and his mouth.

Polenta swore under his breath. Then, in a single breath, he said "Pretty Boy, the Boss wants you to join him with a couple of carving knives to have fun with that asshole, Longhin."

"If you don't mind!" shouted Pagnan.

"What?" asked Polenta.

"You need to add 'If you don't mind'," added Pagnan. By then he had decided to go on with it, humiliating Polenta and indulging in a little display of power.

The Boss liked to brag a bit.

Polenta clenched his teeth. "If you don't mind," he barked.

"OK," confirmed Pretty Boy, then he started to walk towards the other end of the lane holding two shining knives, iron stings ready to bite into Longhin's flesh.

"Aaagh!" Longhin screamed.

Guo didn't understand.

There was no news from Zhang.

And that had consequences. For instance, there was no way he could focus on his speech.

He had decided to practice it from top to bottom, working on each word, trying make his Italian perfect.

He wanted to overshadow all the other speakers and impress the president of the provincial SME confederation, but he was genuinely worried about his nephew. Each time he got to the point where he itemised the ingredients of a spring roll, he stopped and thought about Zhang.

He had decided to use cuisine as an anthropological symbol, as a smart way to compare the two cultures. That was the reason he professed a "fusion" cuisine. He was sure that the SME president would have loved to hear him being so proactive, so open towards local traditions. Comparing tofu and bean soup was a risky thing for sure, but it was also original, a sign of a very open mind.

Even though he was making every effort, he

just couldn't focus: as soon as he paused in his speech to highlight some key passage, Zhang's face appeared in his mind's eye and drew him to a halt.

Also, the signals he had received in the last few hours were not encouraging: no news at all, even though he had insisted on being told as soon as the game with the redhead was over. And worse still, Xan and Wu seemed to have disappeared as well.

It all stunk like rotten seaweed. Guo was afraid that a hole had opened in the perfect structure of the Talking Daggers.

He had a bad feeling that someone was challenging the control he had on that land of failures, a control that was total and complete by now, after years of hard work. And maybe that someone was a dreadlocked redhead. It was only a feeling, of course, but it became more and more unpleasant hour after hour. And the blackout on what had happened to his men did nothing to help him see the matter in a better light.

Guo had made a mistake, only one, but it was unforgivable. This at least was clear. He had trusted an Italian. A useless, stupid *laowai*.

He had decided to give him a chance only because his nephew had insisted. Zhang had told him that he needed to change his way of thinking, to put more trust in the younger generation and that he, Zhang, wanted a chance to be noticed by the whole clan and thus gain their respect.

Guo felt that there was something rotten somewhere. He had caused that crack in the structure of the Talking Daggers clan himself by using inferior material: Ottorino Longhin.

Even though he'd done nothing wrong until then.

He had worked hard, year upon year, to set up a traffic of immigrant slaves, sucking the blood of the *wu ming*, the nameless, the clandestines that travelled from Asia to the garden of delights that is north-east Italy. Thus he had slowly built a small empire.

It had all started when he decided to found the Red Lotus association, officially supporting Chinese immigrants in getting to grips with local bureaucracy – from finding a job and a place to stay, to sorting out all the paperwork – but that was actually a cover for a supermarket of exploitation. By blackmailing the families who were still in China, Guo earned himself thousands and thousands of euros. He asked for twenty thousand for each individual, and those who couldn't or wouldn't pay, quickly became torture fodder.

His men were creative and spared no expense. They beat up each and every new arrival at least until his or her family was prepared to send the money. Then the new immigrant was ready to work for Guo in one of his restaurants in the Veneto countryside or in a bar in the outskirts of Padua or Vicenza. An alternative to being beaten up was to earn their ransom in a sweatshop, locked away in a warehouse with darkened windows, working eighteen-hour shifts.

All of that while sucking the blood of north-east Italy: jeans for fashionable people, five euro rather than twenty-five; shirts for twenty rather than forty. Of course without any of this appearing officially: a dense web of third parties had signed contracts with the major brands that included a veto on subcontracting, a prohibition circumvented by using an army of invisible slaves.

A silent, deadly machine. In Veneto, dozens of entrepreneurs in the textile business had taken their own lives.

Gou had filled the Brenta and Treviso area with his warehouses. He paid his slaves a minimum percentage for each article of clothing they produced, without an hourly wage. Thus he gained an advantage on two fronts: first of all he extended the time they needed to pay their ransom, allowing him to continue employing a pretty much unpaid workforce; also, he forced the *wu ming* to work themselves silly with the fantasy of earning their freedom.

So, little by little, he had deprived Veneto not only of its factories, closing one after another, nearly two hundred every year, but also of its tradition of craftsmanship: the old tailoring schools were starting to disappear, even those that represented the region's oldest heritage.

There it was, globalisation in Chinese sauce.

And those imbecile Italian dickheads hadn't even realised.

And then there were drugs. With the authority coming from his role of White Paper Fan of Triad 14K, Guo was able to re-invest truckloads of money – accumulated by dealing in Double Uoglobe heroin – in the Italian north-east. The purest heroin in the world. Chinese couriers brought it to Paris where it was cut and sent to Amsterdam, to one of the richest and most densely populated Chinatowns in Europe. Little by little, 14K had added the business of cocaine and synthetic drugs to that of heroin. With the unbelievable amount of money thus earned Guo had been able to buy restaurants, bars, shops, warehouses and industrial machinery.

Extorting protection money from the Chinese restaurants that didn't belong to him yet was another method of earning more cash and reducing his competition. Those owners who refused were killed, their bodies burned and hidden somewhere. And they were replaced by a 14K member.

The perfect organisation Guo had set up had until then made sure that his hidden assault on the economy of the Italian north-east hadn't involved any clashes with the judiciary or with local criminal organisations.

That tug-of-war with Pagnan's clan, however, was likely to provoke the situation. Guo was aware that because of his organisation's constant growth, he would sooner or later be forced into some kind of an arrangement with Pagnan's people, but he would have preferred to create an alliance rather than have a direct confrontation.

But he had been completely wrong when he picked a man like Longhin. And now, to make things more complicated, there was that girl.

To employ an Italian had been a breach of the *guanxi*, the relation, that bond of mutual support that linked all the members of the "family" to one another. Not only sons, nephew, cousins and brothers, but everyone who belonged to a much wider group of people from Wenzhou, the area Guo himself came from. *Guanxi* was founded on *li*, the proper ritual behaviour that governs human relationships as a whole, the basis of a thousand year-old social order.

How could he have stooped so low as to make a pact with that damned *laowai*?

Guo was so agitated that he wasn't able to enjoy the piping hot shark fin soup he had been served.

Zou Kai had just called to update him on the failure of their mission: they had not managed to retrieve Longhin, the traitor. They got there too late and now, because of them, the clan was empty-handed. Guo knew that his honour was at stake, in his own mind and in those of all the Talking Daggers. And of course the other Chinese gangs in the Italian north-east would soon notice such a fissure in the structure of his organisation.

The fact that he felt responsible for that disaster wouldn't save Zou Kai from being punished for failure to perform his assigned task. But it was clear to him that such punishment would be pointless, compared to rewinding and going back in time to rectify previous mistakes.

Now he would need to organise some kind of hit to punish Pagnan's gang. One that would leave a mark.

Thinking all that, he lifted the piping cup and started drinking his shark fin soup, gurgling noisily. Its warmth would fix his stomach, aiding what he expected would be a typically troublesome digestion.

Then he picked up a small brass bell, rang it tiredly and waited. A young waiter dressed in white arrived and, in a surreal silence, positioned a teacup bearing the mark of the Ming dynasty, full of hot water, in front of him.

As soon as the waiter had left, Guo fished everything he needed to finally reach a blessed state of relaxation out of a drawer: a disposable syringe with a hypodermic needle, a wad of absorbent cotton, a silver spoon with a curved handle, a half-millimetre soft rubber tourniquet and the most important thing, a transparent bag full of white powder.

He slid over the three-prong silver candle holder that had pride of place on the table. He uncapped the needle and dipped the tip in the hot water. Then he drew the plunger slowly, making sure he stopped the moment the water touched the fifty units mark. He poured the heroin into the spoon and added the water. He lifted the spoon over the blue candle burning on the holder, warming the liquid without allowing it to boil. He removed a small piece of cotton from the wad and placed it on the spoon, waiting for it to soak fully. He then aspirated the solution, hit the needle with his index finger to make sure that the tiny air bubbles inside it escaped and depressed the plunger slightly.

He tied the tourniquet above his left elbow, helping with his teeth, tightened it until the big vein swelled up and inserted the needle.

When he slowly withdrew the plunger a veil of blood appeared lazily inside the syringe. Then, with a firm hit, he injected the heroin, now brown and iron-like due to the contact with his plasma.

The evening air was freezing cold, and the heating in the car was pumping out fire. The shiny blue Ford Focus was speeding angrily through roads built over the ancient Roman borders as if it had a grudge against the asphalt. Mila's eyes were two spots of green jade. Flashing. Feline, ready to snap at its prey.

Having buried the corpses of the two Chinamen in her garden, she'd called Toni "Pudding Man" Carpanese, asking him to go pick up the twins' car with his tow truck, take it to his garage and render it unrecognisable. Toni owned an ice cream shop in Fossalta di Trebaseleghe and, along with his nephew, managed a "free-thinking" garage, one of those in which even a Fiat 127 that should have been scrapped could pass an official vehicle inspection test. He picked up the Mercedes without any questions.

Mila was driving towards Pagnan's bowling

alley. Ten to one the fat man had sent someone to pick the traitor up so he could grill him like a sausage to find out who he had sold out to.

She was reasonably certain that she'd find the whole gang gathered in that white elephant in the middle of the Massanzago countryside.

If they weren't there she would go to Pagnan's villa. She had studied that old walrus' habits too thoroughly to be mistaken. He was as predictable as a cheating husband.

The Veneto countryside flew past the windows. The severed heads of the two Chinese killers rolled around in the boot like a bag of footballs.

Mila crossed the Massanzago main street without slowing down and, just past the village, saw a road sign for the bowling alley. She took a side road and, after a couple of bends, reached a huge space where the fields gave way to an enormous parking lot, completely empty except for a cobalt blue Audi A3 and a black BMW X5, Rossano Pagnan's very own car.

Mila parked, respecting the lines drawn on the lot, extracted Zhang's mobile phone and selected the last number in the list of outgoing calls.

Guo Xiaoping's, no doubt.

A voice, old but strong, answered after seven rings.

"Mr Guo?"

"Who's there?"

"Mr Guo, my name is Mila Zago. Your nephew has been following me all day. If it helps you to place me, my hair is red, dreadlocked."

"You killed my nephew, madam?" asked Guo.

"No, better than that. I neutralised him. Now he's my hostage."

The man breathed out.

"True words are not eloquent, eloquent words are not true," he added.

"I don't think I understand."

"I was quoting Laozi. Good move, anyway."

"You shouldn't have had me followed, Mr Guo."

"Clearly."

"Men often underestimate women."

"A mistake I personally avoid making."

"Good for you. Your nephew was not so careful. Now, Mr Guo, I have a suggestion for you."

"Tell me."

"Please bear with me a minute, so I can explain how things stand right now."

Once he had reached Ottorino Longhin, who was trembling like a leaf in autumn, Pretty Boy smiled and slid his knives against one another with the skill of a traditional armourer. He was going to skin his victim like a chicken when something stopped him.

"Boss!" A high-pitched, slightly insane-sounding voice, like a young, eager, considerate aunt. It was Giacomo Manzan, known as the Newbie, who was keeping watch at the door. Manzan was a strapping lad, flesh and muscle toned by regular gym sessions. His head, very small compared to the rest of his body, was shaven, smooth as a snooker ball.

"What now?" shouted Pagnan, fearing that the Mayor of Muson might appear out of the blue followed by the parish priest and some horses to give him a ready-made speech about children, horses, ponies and parents.

Then he looked up and understood.

Outside the bowling alley, in front of the door, he saw the dreadlocked redhead. The killer.

She was walking in black boots, swaying her hips like a panther, sheathed in leather trousers moulded over her round, muscular hips, a figure-hugging light blue top.

Silver bracelets on her forearms, full red lips, nearly fluorescent green eyes all suggested an Amazon that could easily become a Fury.

Two Colt .45s with a mother-of-pearl stock in her shoulder holsters were a pretty persuasive sight for anyone. She was carrying a burlap sack, heavily stained with blood.

"What now, you ask? I have the answer to all your questions," Mila said. Her dark, slightly hoarse voice sounded arrogant to the men in the bowling alley.

"What answers would I be looking for? And who are you? The Virgin Mary?" replied Pagnan, inflating his belly as if he was trying to make his already enormous bulk seem even larger.

"Yeah, who the fuck do you think you are, Miss Know-it-all?" added Mule. He had set his eyes on her the very instant she entered. He wanted to put her over his knee and give her a spanking, but couldn't quite work out why.

"Shut up, child, and be quiet. You might get hurt with a babysitter like me." Mila smiled back at him. "I'm waiting for you to give me a reason to put a couple of holes in your stomach so that everyone can see what you ate for breakfast."

"Phew," whistled Pretty Boy. "She's going to kick your ass, Mule! Be careful, she has a temper on her."

"Stop this bullshit and let's get back to the original question, baby." Pagnan wanted to cut to the chase. His position forced him to.

Mila didn't reply. She kept striding forward until she got into the middle of the gangsters.

"Here's your answer," said Mila, and upturned

the burlap sack, dropping its macabre contents right on the white foul line.

The severed heads fell with a thump. Two rotten watermelons leaking a reddish juice.

Pagnan froze, Pretty Boy uttered a hoarse "Ah!" with some admiration. Tripe nearly choked on his soup. Polenta's eyes goggled, as did Mule's. The Newbie yelped, reaching an incredible pitch. A symphony of astonishment swept over those six hardasses, stunned by the redhead's theatrics.

"Christ, what the fuck is it, the head of John the Baptist? And where are the bodies? Did you eat them?" Pagnan was proud of his sense of humour. It never let him down.

"Your man betrayed you for a gang of Chinamen. Simple and sad," Mila said. "Then again, seeing how much they pay, you can't really blame him. People from Veneto are famous for being pretty miserable, am I right?" Her question wavered like an offhand jibe.

"Hey, fuck off, kid. Don't think you can come here and insult me. This is my playing field and if you piss me off I can get you thrown out! With a whole bunch of broken bones, for fuck's sake!" Pagnan was starting to lose his temper.

"Just give me the green light and I'll deal with her," added Mule with fiery eyes.

"Hey, hey, boys, easy… is this how you treat a

lady? I came in peace. I even brought you the heads of your enemies; you should thank me, not insult me."

"Well, actually," Tripe said, "she's not wrong."

"Shut up! When I want your opinion, I'll ask for it. Keep eating your vile shit and leave me the fuck alone, Tripe!" Then, moving his stare back towards Mila, Pagnan changed the tone of his voice. "OK, *mademoiselle*, you're not wrong. Let's start again. Fancy a drink? I'm thirsty. We could sit at that table down there and have a word, just so I can try to understand who you are, what you're doing here and what it is you want."

# 7

Guo felt better now.

At least he could plan his next move.

And there was still hope he'd come out of the situation a winner after all.

He was furious, of course.

But his head was clear.

He knew he needed to act immediately. He had all the information he needed.

Pagnan had managed to retrieve Ottorino Longhin, snatched him from under his nose like a fish in a net. Zhang had fallen into a trap because he had proven to be incompetent. His profession didn't allow mistakes, and Zhang had made far too many. Now he had paid for them.

Guo had tried to warn him more than once, but his stupid nephew had not wanted to understand, just kept steamrolling down his own path. And at the end of that path, Mila Zago had been waiting to close his account.

But the girl could end up being a formidable ally. She had started feeding him useful information. He thought about it. He could reap the benefits now and then turn the tables on her later. With a little luck he'd be able to destroy Pagnan, acquire control over the whole criminal society in north-eastern Italy and have a deadly killer on hand, a killer who at the right moment he could turn into a scapegoat for what would surely end up being a bloody massacre. Mila Zago needed to be punished for what she had done, but in the meantime he could usefully exploit her.

According to what the girl had told him, Pagnan was currently busy torturing Longhin somewhere in the countryside. In order to second-guess him, Guo needed to organise an attack on his arch enemy's villa, which wasn't guarded at the moment. Maybe the rest of his family were there, and he could kill them all. His wife and his kids. So that Pagnan, blind with rage, would go looking for him. And when he did, he'd find Guo lying in wait. And once he'd captured him, Guo would cook him nice and slowly, over a low flame.

With those thoughts on his mind, Guo dialled a number on his mobile phone.

Five rings, no answer.

Finally, after twelve rings, a voice answered. Zou Kai's voice. Guo gave him a series of instructions and promised that if he completed them successfully, Guo might reconsider the situation Zou Kai and his men were in.

Zou Kai thanked him respectfully.

Guo ended the call.

"So, how did you get here?"

"Well, I know the bowling alley belongs to you. I mean, it wasn't a huge effort on my part. Everyone around here knows," replied Mila, looking into Pagnan's eyes.

"That right?"

"Sure is."

"Let's say you're right. How could you be sure I was here?"

"I couldn't. I just thought there'd be a fair chance."

"OK, OK. Fancy a drink?" Pagnan called Pretty Boy who meanwhile had put his knives aside, certain they wouldn't be needed again that evening.

"A margarita. With strawberries," said Mila.

"Good girl. Pretty Boy, mix two of those. Lots of ice, lots of salt."

Tripe and Polenta had moved closer to the table where Pagnan and Mila were sitting.

From the far end of the lane Longhin wasn't making a sound, quieter than a hibernating tortoise.

Mule was staring at Mila as if he was about to eat her at any moment.

"So, Big Man, let's cut to the chase. I killed two Chinamen and am holding a third hostage. All from Guo's gang. Same guys who made all that mess at Limenella Nord with your former flunkey."

"My, my," said Pagnan. "You're very well informed!"

"I know more, if you're interested."

"Really?"

"Really."

"Like what?"

"Well, I know Guo paid Longhin to kill your accountants in a service station on the motorway. That he stole two million from you. And that you're scared of him."

"Are you joking? I can eat that yellow ape for breakfast. My revenge will be giving him so much shit that he'll turn black overnight."

"Hmm... maybe so. But the fact that he's the

leader of a Chinese gang deeply rooted here in the north-east and linked to a powerful triad such as 14K, well, I'm thinking that could be an issue for you, and you know it. Also, I know where your two million is, and you don't."

"You certainly do know a lot of stuff... sweetie. I just realised I don't know your name, you never told me. You know a lot about me and I know jack shit about you. And that's not good, sweetie."

"You can call me Mila," she said, caressing her red dreadlocks with her right hand. Her hair shone like fire in the blinding neon light.

"What a shitty name," said Pagnan. "It sounds like a yogurt. Come on, tell me your real name."

"Mila *is* my real name. Anyway, believe it or not, that's up to you, Big Man."

"Stop calling me 'Big Man'."

"Right y'are, Big Man."

Pagnan burst out in a fat laugh. He liked this girl. She had balls like a bull's and some backbone, much more than any of his men.

"Anyway," Mila carried on, "if you accept my offer and if you're really not afraid, I'll sort out the Chinese for you."

"Really?"

"Sure. I'm a professional killer after all. The best you ever saw, I've no doubt. Nobody owns me, but for the right money I'm ready to clear the place of your yellow friends."

"How can I be sure you're not full of crap?"

"Those two severed heads are an initial guarantee. The second is the hostage. And he's not just any hostage. I'm talking about Guo's nephew. Guo will do all he can to get him back home, you can bet on it. Plus, as far as I'm concerned you can take all the credit for yourself. Strengthen your reputation as a merciless leader heading a gang of crazy killers, so nobody will ever mess with you again. And you'll be able to manage your business in perfect freedom, with no competition. Of course I don't come cheap, but we'll talk about that later. Just to make sure I won't have any trouble at the end of it all, I'm the only one who knows where your money is. And until I'm sure I can trust you, that'll be my life insurance."

While they'd been talking, Pretty Boy had brought them two Margaritas, filled to the brim. The salt covering the edges of the glasses looked like snow even though it was roasting in the bowling alley. Seconds later he came back with a glass bowl full of big, red strawberries.

"Hmm, let's see," said Pagnan. "We can put you to the test, see what you can do. Sure, you know where the money is. But blackmail isn't a great way to make me trust you. Then again, how do I know you're not bluffing?"

"Whatever. But first of all you have to find someone to kill me, and I can't see anyone in here who's up to the job; and then, of course, if you kill me you lose your last chance to get your two million back. Yes, maybe I am bluffing. But what if I'm not? Trust me, you'll end up thanking me."

"Right, right. I still have the feeling that you're overestimating yourself, but the fact remains, you've killed two of the yellow fuckers and have a third hostage."

At which point, Mule couldn't restrain himself any longer and spoke up.

"Boss, can I say something before this little girl is officially enrolled?"

"Sure."

"Well, we can't trust her. Who knows where she got those heads? Who knows if she has the balls for the job? If something goes wrong you'll end up looking like a right twat, boss. Those fucking rice-eaters will think you've gone soft."

"Well, Mule, it doesn't look like you guys have done that awesome a job up until now," Mila teased him while biting into a huge strawberry.

"Fuck off, bitch! What the fuck do you want from us? Think you can come here and hurl abuse at us, eh? Think you're so smart? Boss, I don't want this little brat here in my fucking way."

"Since when is what you want more important than what I decide?" exploded Pagnan. "She's not completely wrong, you know. We did do a crappy job. When I called you to tell you what had happened you were completely baffled. None of you had even suspected what that son of a bitch down there at the other end of the lane was plotting behind my back. You're all useless pieces of shit!"

"But boss…" moaned Tripe.

"Shut up! Shut up, all of you! You made a fucking arse of picking up a fucking traitor. And the facts are that fucking Guo killed the two best accountants in Veneto and stole two million euro from me. I'll give the girl a chance, cause she's the only one who's scored any points for our team. Mule, you'll be her shadow. You'll eat with her, take a dump with her, walk with her… but don't fuck her. Am I clear?"

"Clear. What about the heads?" replied Mule.

"I can deliver them to Guo in some pretty wrapping paper," suggested Mila.

"Great idea! Mule can go with you. And you should go straight away. To that fucking Chinese restaurant he owns in Cadoneghe. Mule, tell him the heads were your doing. I want to see that fucking rice-eater fry like one of his disgusting ice cream fritters."

"I'll propose a truce and arrange a meeting between you," Mila added.

"Why? What for?"

"It makes sense," she replied with a smile, "if on the day of the meeting I'm five hundred yards away with a sniper rifle to take out all the Chinese. You'll only need to make sure I have a clear shot and then take cover so I can kill them all."

"Brilliant idea."

"I think so."

"Fine. Now let me drink this fucking Margarita."

"Boss, one final detail," Pretty Boy said.

"What the fuck is it now?"

"Longhin. What do you want us to do with him?"

"Longhin? Ah, right. Shoot him."

# 8

*From Mila Zago's journal:*

Rossano Pagnan was under investigation
for incitement to murder, an offence valid
when it's proven that the defendant
"incited or induced to act" the person who
committed the crime. To be clear, the
subject must have instigated or provoked
the criminal intent in someone else.

That's what Pagnan's lawyer mouthed
into journalists' microphones on the day
his client was set free. He was spouting
forth with that crystal clear voice of his,
wearing a bow tie and a linen suit. I

watched it on television. Dozens of times. I felt utter hatred towards him when he gave the cameras one of his best smiles.

I hadn't understood exactly what he was talking about. But it was clear to me that his ludicrous speech pattern, full of legal jargon, would have stuck in our throats. And above all it would have been what saved Pagnan.

I should have expected it to end up like that. The Public Prosecutor, after having talked more than once to each witness during the preliminary investigations, had decided that the evidence to support the accusation of incitement to murder was not enough and had himself asked for Pagnan to be released from prison.

So, a fish always stinks from the head down. Isn't that what they say? And everything in that story sounded dubious, even before the avalanche of bullshit began.

Luckily the judge rejected the request for Pagnan's release, explaining the existence of the incitement to murder charge with a series of facts: Pagnan and the killers were close friends, and the relations between the subjects suggested with a reasonable

certainty the existence of a criminal
conspiracy. Further elements supporting
the accusation had later appeared thanks to
the investigations conducted by my father
before he was murdered. Investigations
that, according to the judge, had caused his
death.

But it was not enough. Can you believe
that? Shit! Pagnan's lawyer didn't give up.
He insisted that the motivations given by
the judge, besides not having precedents,
could open a path to a very dangerous
legal interpretation: contributory
negligence to be pinned on anyone
unlucky enough to be friends with a
person who has committed a crime.

In my opinion it was much more
straightforward: the Public Prosecutor was
on Pagnan's books. You can't be the
number one criminal in Veneto if you're
unable to corrupt the right people at the
right time. Everybody was aware of the
relationship between Rossano Pagnan and
Saverio Donolato, aka Mule. Where one
went, the other followed. And my father
had been investigating Rossano Pagnan for
quite a while. The judges and the police
knew, they damn well knew.

Our defending counsel, Mr Carraro, told us to stay confident as the preliminary judge was on our side – or rather on the side of Truth.

But I didn't believe him and more importantly I couldn't wait.

It felt like living through another nightmare. Not only was my father dead, but I also had to listen to an asshole in a linen suit pontificating to the world while he tried to get Pagnan sprung from jail.

I tried to unwind by training. In the afternoons, in the evenings, all the time. I'd run mile after mile, I'd have the longest gym sessions imaginable, crazy stuff.

One day, after a first run, I got to the fourth station in the fitness trail. The Brenta was swaying, soft and slow, under the sun. I'd gone to ground on my back, my legs under a log so I could train my abs, when a disgusting, sickly sweet smell assaulted my nostrils. A rank, pulsating whiff that dominated the air. An obscene, violent, unbearable smell. I moved my legs from under the log, stood up, looked around.

Then I saw it.

Someone had nailed a toad to one end of

the log. Its body was now a brown slush, blood and guts leaking out of its small belly, deflated like a punctured ball.

They had made a thorough job, those bastards. After gutting it, they'd used it as a pincushion. Who the fuck would enjoy doing something like that? I remained there, my mouth gaping and my eyes wide open staring at that little, mangled body.

An icy sadness coursed through me. I closed my eyes and remained there, on my feet, without moving, crying silent tears and facing the blood-red dusk.

It was as if I had seen my father's tragedy reflected in that small, dead animal. Trampled on and nails driven into him in life and memory. Crucified and displayed in the public square so people could spit on him.

Grandpa went to and fro between home and the lawyer's office. Most of the time he came back empty-handed. He insisted on being seen every day, as if Carraro was able to focus only on our trial. Now I believe he was using it as an excuse to have something to do every day in order to exorcise the frustration that was increasing daily.

At the end of the investigation the Public

Prosecutor applied for the case to be dismissed. Carraro opposed the request, and his opposition was accepted. But at the following hearing the judge delivered a verdict of non-suit.

Which meant that Pagnan, that fucker, got out of jail with his police record still immaculate.

It all ended in such a sad, pathetic kind of way. When I think back to those days I feel an overwhelming rage. I want to break everything around me.

My father had ended up in the gutter in this fucking town, and nobody had lifted a finger to help.

Many said that the judgement was a scandal, an insult to the law. Stupid, damned, useless words.

I still remember Mr Carraro's face as he tried to explain what had happened. He couldn't understand how the system had cheated us so badly. He cried.

That was what hurt me most. I looked at him, in his sober and refined office, bent over his oak desk. His hands desperately crumpling his paperwork.

I was still staring at the documents, the acts, the enormous folders, unable to believe. That sea of paper evoked only a feeling of impotence. In silence, Grandpa put an arm around my shoulders. Grandma had long since run out of tears.

Everything had happened "in the name of the law".

I was studying Law. I realised once more how pointless it was to study a system of rules that has completely failed.

Because it is managed by human beings.

Nothing will ever persuade me that most of those who could have spoken out or done something to help, didn't do so because they were on Pagnan's books. Including the Public Prosecutor and the preliminary trial judge.

After all, why did the judge who accepted our objection die a year later in a very suspicious car crash?

In my opinion human beings are incapable of getting close to justice. Not even a little bit.

What should a girl think when her mother doesn't want her, her father is murdered, she gets raped and the person behind the murder is free, plotting his next criminal enterprise?

That's why I decided to become who I am.

That's why my only objective is to punish Pagnan. I can't stand the idea that he is allowed to breathe the same air that normal people breathe. It just doesn't make sense. As long as I have the strength, as long as I still breathe, I will live only to hunt him down – him and the people like him. To flush those pieces of shit out of their hidey-holes, embodying a superhuman strength that causes fear, panic, despair.

The strength of a Fury.

Strong-arm tactics.

An eye for an eye.

A tooth for a tooth.

Those are the only words I know. The only words that work. Because there must be something rotten in us. The civilization we built has deprived us of a sense of justice, of ethics, of dignity to the extent that we don't even know what those words mean anymore. We fill our mouths with words such as politics, transaction, parole, rehabilitation, reduction of sentence, statute of limitation, pardon. The good guys and the bad guys don't exist any longer, they're all mentally ill now. Of unsound mind, "inciter to a crime" at a

stretch: what does "inciter to a crime"
mean? One who assists without acting but
rather instigates, favours, promotes a
criminal deed.

So what?

Once they called them instigators, that
was it.

But the instigator is the scariest of all.
He's the one who can cause more crimes. I
mean, who is more powerful, an
entrepreneur or a factory worker? Easy
answer I think.

Rossano Pagnan is still alive, at liberty.
He gets richer, he steals, he deals drugs, he
orders murders, he pimps. But he hides it
all with a mountain of money, he lines his
disgusting life with banknotes and makes
eyes and mouths close at his whim.
Everyone's mouths. He owns the best
lawyers, the best accountants, the best
whores. They all do the same job, and
they're great at it.

My father lies under the ground.

Murdered in a shoot-out because he was
upholding the law. He was serving the
country.

And what did the country do for him?

Did it give him justice?

Did it punish those responsible for his death?

Did it reward him for having defended the order and the values that are supposed to be the foundation of our country itself?

Like fuck it did!

I promised myself, in front of a mirror, that I would no longer feel fear, no longer allow mercy. For me they now are empty words, spent words, worn out, melted away.

I will be Fury and Torment.

I will enjoy the pain I inflict on those who caused pain.

I will feed on this. My cruelty will be my strength. And the more I am able to mutilate, torture, crush, cut, destroy, murder, the more my smile will become sweet, sparkling.

An eye for an eye.

A tooth for a tooth.

# 9

Guo had withdrawn to the quiet of the relaxation room, where he used to go to smoke a cigar or read a book.

Just a few minutes earlier he had talked with the president of the local SME confederation to agree the minutiae of his short speech on cultural integration. That had helped cheer him up.

He was enjoying the feeling of being on the right path when Xing, the waiter, announced visitors.

Ah, she was here. Guo was more than curious to see this woman in the flesh. But he played it cool.

He gave a tired glance at the wonderful teak panels that covered the walls of the room.

Delicate watercolours hung there, illuminated by the soft light of brass lamps with silk shades. On the smooth stone floor was a striking sky blue carpet; at each corner, a golden embroidered dragon clawed at the planet Earth, placed in the centre of the carpet like an ancestral seal.

"Sir…" said Xing.

"What?"

"A foxy-looking girl and a bloke who looks like one of those local gangsters want to talk to you."

"To me?"

"Yes, sir."

"Since when do people think they can talk to me?"

"I don't know, sir."

"A girl, you say?"

"Yes, sir."

"Foxy?"

"Yes, sir."

"What do you mean by 'foxy', Xing?"

"Well, she's wearing tight-fitting clothes and has quite striking red hair."

"Have they been searched?"

"Of course, sir."

"Were they carrying?"

"Both of them, but not any longer."

"Let them in."

"OK, sir."

"Properly escorted, of course."

"Of course."

"I wonder why I always need to do everything myself."

"Very well, sir."

"Screw your 'very well', Xing."

"Thank you, sir."

After only a few seconds, a girl walked in through the big central door that led from the dining room to the relaxation room, a girl that even old Guo considered very good looking, followed closely by one of those blasted locals in a dark blue suit, his teeth mostly gold, watery eyes, bright like the sky, and a protruding chin.

To complete the procession, three of his men: Zeng, Lin and Quingguo. Two positioned themselves at either side of Guo, one behind Mila and Mule.

Mila stared at the three men as they took their positions. Took off her leather jacket and tied it around her waist, then dropped the burlap sack she was holding in her right hand.

The thud of the sack was sinister.

"Good evening, Mr Guo," said Mila.

"Good evening," replied Guo, his dark eyes staring at the girl with curiosity while he softly touched his silver but still thick hair.

Guo already knew how it would end.

"So, Mr Guo, I'll not waste anyone's time," Mila added. "As you're about to see with your own eyes, this sack contains the heads of two of your men."

The Chinaman didn't even flinch as the heads of Xan and Wu rolled out of the sack like two balls, stained with coagulated blood.

Zou Kai and Tonk Liy were running like hell.

Two Rottweilers were catching up on them. Black, huge, monstrous.

A crying child was watching the scene from the door.

The wall surrounding the villa seemed far away, unreachable for the two sprinting Chinamen, when they noticed a cherry-red Seat Leon parked on one of the paths in the garden.

An unexpected glimmer of hope. They just managed to get in and close the door before the dogs reached them. Jaws wide open, the dogs started prowling around the car in which those juicy meals were locked, prowling like things possessed.

Zou Kai and Tonk looked each other in the eye and started to scream, then they started to empty the magazines of their guns at the beasts.

The bullets bounced off the glass like olive stones thrown at an unbreakable mirror, ricocheting everywhere.

"Stop!" Zou Kai shouted.

They were lucky not to get hit.

Fucking bulletproof glass.

They should have thought of that. It was one of Pagnan's cars, after all.

Zou Kai looked for the keys, but couldn't find them.

While he was still searching for them, he heard the doors being locked.

Clack!

Central locking.

Tonk's hand gripped his shoulder.

Zou Kai raised his eyes. On his friend's face was an expression of pure terror.

Then Tonk nodded towards the house.

Zou Kai saw a series of terrifying images: the locked windows, the dogs preparing to devour them, the grass under the pitch black sky, the vast distance both from the wall and from the house and... and the face of a child.

Who was the child? Where had he come from? They hadn't noticed any children in the house. And why was he holding something that looked a lot like an ignition key?

The child was smiling.

He was smiling because he had screwed them over.

Zou Kai tried to close and reopen his eyes. The child was still there. Holding them by the balls.

They had just massacred everyone in Pagnan's house, Tonk and him had. Like old mental Guo, bloodthirsty as ever, had ordered.

It had been an execution, not without gory special effects. They'd really gone to town on this job.

Unfortunately the one thing a professional killer who has just finished turning his (or her) enemy's family into a bloody pulp can never afford to do is to stay in their house.

Unbelievable! They were at the mercy of a smiling little gnome who they had stupidly failed to spot. And who was now taunting them.

When they entered the villa they'd only seen the woman and the Filipino waiter and had slaughtered them immediately. After trashing the house, decorating the walls with ideograms and Triad symbols, ruining the floors and ripping up the curtains, they'd left the same way they went in. But, as soon as they crossed the armoured door towards the garden, they had heard the dogs' angry barking and started running like men possessed.

Their sudden flight had not allowed them to think clearly. That garden gnome had probably been hiding under the bed or somewhere. They'd missed him and now they were going to pay for it.

"We're fucked," said Zou Kai.

"Why do you say that?" asked Tonk, who was clearly hoping for some supernatural intervention.

It was a stupid question. So stupid that Zou Kai decided to vent his considerable frustration in his reply. "What don't you understand? When Pagnan and his men come back, it'll be a total clusterfuck. As soon as he sees what we've done, he'll be furious. He'll be happy to drag us out of here and torture us for days on end, ripping out our organs one at a time. You know what I think? We should kill ourselves. At least that way we get to screw them over."

"We decided to resolve the issue with them, old man – your nephew and your friends. So, if you weren't aware of it yet, you'll see now that Rossano Pagnan is someone you better not fuck with," said Mule who wanted to make his entrance with words intended for effect.

"And who would you be, sir?"

"I'm the one who'll squeeze your testicles in a vice, Mr Guo."

"Damn, I'm quivering like a hare in a net."

"Yes, right. Make all your ping pong jokes, you'll see how it ends."

Mila observed the elderly Chinaman's steady gaze as he stared at the severed heads of his men lying on the floor. Guo's lips seemed to be cracking in a faint smile. She was just a little impressed. "You don't seem too bothered, but those are the heads of two of your men – aren't they?" she said.

Guo nodded slightly.

"You're not wrong. Point is, deep inside I knew it would end up like this. I'm simply realising that my darkest expectations have come true."

"Well done, old man, so please realise that something else might happen – or rather, has already happened. We have your nephew. He's alive at the moment, but we plan to shorten his lifespan as soon as possible," added Mule. He felt the urge to pick up the Chinaman and shake him, he was so cold and apparently deprived of any feeling. Mule would have liked to wipe that frozen turkey expression off his face.

"Words are like pearls: rare and precious. You talk too much, boy. Calm down or what may happen in the short term is that my men will… how do you say it… riddle you with bullets."

Mule's face turned purple and he started to move, but Mila grabbed his wrist. After all, they were there to reach an agreement.

The old man started to talk again.

"I am not particularly affected by the news that you've taken my nephew. I knew in my heart that that silly boy was never going to get anywhere. He is not aware of his traditions, of his history. Just like you, you don't know anything about your people and have forgotten everything. This betrayal of your people's memory is the first sign of your impending defeat."

Mule puffed out his shoulders. The Chinaman was speaking like a book and he – a die-hard fan of Bonelli's action comic books and sensational declamations – felt a little lost. He was in a position of power, but the Chinaman didn't seem to realise it or, worse still, had no intention of acknowledging the fact.

Guo nodded towards his men.

The three henchmen extracted their guns. Semiautomatic Glock .17s loaded with 9mm Parabellum bullets.

"Sir, madam, please tell me your names and then we'll sit and have a drink. I'll tell you a story, even if you don't want to listen. Because, you see, what you will hear is not only the best possible explanation for my behaviour, but also a most effective warning for the future."

This further taunt from the Chinaman made Mule roll his eyes. He couldn't cope with it, he was not prepared to cope with a talkative, pompous Asian. He hated people who thought they were God Almighty, and this one could be the honorary president of the Association of Asian Windbags. But, summoning all his patience, he managed to avoid an outburst and spit out the reply Guo was waiting for.

"You can call me Mule, and this is already more than you need to know. I'll have a Zacapa rum, if you have some."

"Mila. No drinks for me," added his companion.

Old Guo called the waiter and ordered the Zacapa rum for Mule and some rice grappa for himself. The three henchmen put their Glocks away, ready to draw them again if either of the guests so much as yawned.

Mila and Mule sat at the two ends of a comfortable couch decorated in blue designs that matched the carpet.

Guo nestled on a plain leather chair and started talking.

"The story I want to tell you is about the country I come from: China. And explains why we see things a certain way. But let's start from the beginning. I'll tell you about the origins of the great secret society: the Triad. Its name is inspired by the basic idea of traditional Chinese philosophy: Sky, Earth and Man. History tells us that the last Emperor of the Ming dynasty,

Chongzhen, took his own life. He hanged himself
to avoid being taken by the Manchurian Qing,
barbaric people who in 1644 invaded the Empire
and overthrew the most radiant dynasty in China,
silencing it. But the Ming were not dead like the
invaders from Manchu in the north had thought.
And in the late seventeenth century a bloody
uprising reddened the Chinese lands once more,
thanks to a group of warrior monks, the Shaolin
Tigers: a hundred and twenty-eight martial arts
masters who led the rebellion against their bitter
rivals. The Tigers were based in a monastery built
many centuries before in Henan, on the north
face of Mount Songshan. But the Qing army was
too big and too well organised to be defeated by
those heroes. So, still according to legend, in 1736
they razed the monastery and massacred the
Shaolin Tigers.

"But not all of them died. Five survived and
fled, settling in different areas of China. From
there they started teaching the five Shaolin
Wushu animal plays: leopard, tiger, snake, crane
and dragon. The first of them, called *bao quan*, is
practiced to develop physical strength. The
second, *hu quan*, makes bones, thighs and waist
stronger. A constant training of all the joints
makes the body sturdier and sturdier. The third,
*she quan*, is focused on developing vital energy

and inner strength, or *qi*, to give the body the flexibility and rhythmic stamina that characterise snakes. The fourth, *he quan*, improves harmony, self-control and inner peace, all very important in defeating an enemy. And finally *long quan*, the dragon, which strengthens the spirit. One who masters those five techniques will be an undefeatable warrior. Now, back to the legend of the birth of the Triad, it is important to remember that those monks, besides the techniques I just described, spread the idea of rebellion against the Qing, and from that the first secret societies – and, later, the Triad – were born."

"You ever going to get to the punchline, you old bastard?" asked Mule who felt impelled to interrupt that river of words.

Guo smiled.

Mila kept staring at the old man like a child hanging onto every word from her grandfather's lips while he tells her a story.

"Patience. Keep listening and hear what happened. And learn something, if you can. Amongst all the secret societies that were created in those days one rose above the others in importance: Hong, from the name of the first Ming Emperor – Hong Hui. The society picked as its symbol a triangle, or Triad, representing the elements of Sky, Earth and Man. To quote Laozi,

'The way generates One, One generates Two, Two generates the Triad, and the Triad generates everything'. Years later, in 1912, Sun Yat-sen's revolution put an end to the Manchurian government of the Qing. Hong was the main financial supporter of the revolution and finally reached its goal, in remembrance of which every prospective member of the Triad still needs to repeat the motto 'Destroy the Qing to restore the Ming'."

"Seems like just a stupid tongue-twister to me," joked Mule, "and I still don't understand why you're keeping us here listening to all this bullshit."

"I see that your manners are not improving, Mr Mule. I doubt that you will learn anything from what I said. Maybe Miss Mila will show better judgement and understand the meaning of this story. Anyway, I'm tired of your rudeness."

Guo looked at the man standing behind his guests.

The man walked around Mule and hit him on the mouth with the butt of his gun.

"Aargh!" screamed Mule while the Chinaman added a left jab to the face.

Pagnan's right hand man was struggling to breathe, blood flowing from his nose and lips.

"Give Mr Mule a handkerchief, I don't want the floor to get stained."

Mila stared at the old patriarch, eyes full of respect. She started to understand why these people had managed to impose themselves on the social fabric of wherever they settled down: they felt they belonged to a bigger picture, and because of that they had been able to create an efficient and ruthless organisation that could destroy all obstacles. That was exactly what was happening in Veneto. Anyway, she remained silent, waiting for Guo to finish his story, completely ignoring Mule.

"When Communism arrived, Hong, which had meanwhile spawned many more Triads including the American Tong, moved to Hong Kong island." Guo continued after swallowing a couple of sips of his rice grappa, "From that day onwards it became the real fatherland of Chinese secret societies. Each Triad is a complex structure split into several ranks, from its leader, the Dragon Head or *San Fu*, to an immense army of foot soldiers. To each rank is assigned a number divisible by three, and each new member needs to prove they know the thirty-six strategies and the thirty-six oaths. In the past an initiation ceremony could take several hours. But nowadays it's reduced to drawing some blood from a finger of the new member and reading the thirty-six oaths and the key motto of the Triad:

'Destroy the Qing to restore the Ming'. The biggest Triad is 14K, which was born and flourished in Hong Kong along with what used to be its eight sisters. In 1944, in Hong Kong, there were nine main Triads: Wo, Rung, Tung, Chuen, Shing, Fuk Yee Hing, Yee On, 14K and Luen. 14K was the most violent, merciless and terrible, but it was because of this that, despite being persecuted and hunted down, it was the one that grew the most, and now has tens of thousands of members all over the world."

Guo took one more break. Drank some more rice grappa then fixed his ice-cold stare on Mila and then, for a longer time, on Mule.

"See, 14K is the Triad I belong to, and this is why – besides being proud of it and of my brothers – I am not afraid of you. The history of 14K is legendary and it doesn't matter if a bunch of Veneto farmers start cutting the heads off my men. Of course this doesn't mean I'm not interested in having my nephew back, as he might be stupid but he's also blood of my blood. Anyway, his ignorance and your bravado won't be able to put a dent in the great tradition of 14K."

Mule stared at the old man with eyes full of hate, but after the treatment he'd received earlier he decided to remain quietly sitting on the couch.

Mila spoke.

"Mr Guo," she said, "we thank you for this valuable lesson. You're right: if we locals were more aware of where we came from, maybe it would be easier for us to band together. To band together to uphold certain values, maybe, or simply against your people."

Guo nodded with a smile.

"Still, Mule and I are here for a specific reason, besides making you aware of the enormous sadness Mr Rossano Pagnan feels for the death of his two accountants. The reason we're here is to propose a meeting with Mr Pagnan in order to find a satisfactory agreement on the division of territory between your two organisations so you can both go about your activities unhindered."

"You speak with care and respect for your interlocutor, Mila. I congratulate you," said Guo.

"I speak the way I speak. Anyway, that doesn't change anything. We know for certain that you're a White Paper Fan for 14K, which means you're in charge of financial and administrative matters for the Triad. We also know that you're here to develop the network of the Talking Daggers – a gang that's nothing more than your personal plaything, even if it is formally affiliated to 14K. Exploitation of illegal immigrants, money laundering, drug dealing, currency smuggling, counterfeit goods: those are only a few of the activities in your small criminal empire. Don't think we don't know."

"Edzactly!" added Mule.

"And we are perfectly aware of how important your nephew Zhang is to you. And, by the way, you just confirmed it. Your blood relation is as important as your entrepreneurial – so to speak – interests. I'm not a Triad member but I have an idea of how much blood matters in Chinese society. You'll never admit it in front of us, but the truth is you can't wait to be told how and where to meet Pagnan so you can reach an agreement and get your nephew back."

"Edzactly," confirmed Mule, like a broken record.

"I like you, Mila," said Guo pompously, "and I don't deny that it would be interesting for me to consider having you as my right-hand person."

"Aah, eben the old man is droking your ego now, eh Mila?" said Mule.

"Don't bother, Mr Mule," continued Guo. "Anyway, Mila, I agree that a meeting would be worth considering. Where do you plan to hold it?"

"In the Badda," interrupted Mule.

"Where?"

"I think he means the Bassa, the lowland territory in the south of the Province."

"Yed."

"The Bassa?"

"Yed, yed!"

"Where exactly? You see, my friends, I know perfectly what the Bassa is. Knowing your territory and everything about it and yourselves, of course, is vital in enabling me to cause you trouble, but I'd need a slightly more precise location."

"On the road to Badia Polesine," said Mila. "Leave the A13 at the Rovigo exit, and from there follow the signs to Lendinara. Then follow road number 88 and, when you get to the sign welcoming you to Badia Polesine, take a dirt road on the right, through the fields. Drive on past an old abandoned furnace until you reach the yard of an old farmhouse. There you'll find Pagnan's car waiting for you."

"Fine, Mila."

"Tomorrow evening, 5 sharp."

"I'll be there."

"Good. So will Rossano Pagnan."

"I hope so. And I also hope that my nephew will be there. Otherwise, please be warned: my response will be quite terrifying."

"Frankly, Mr Guo, I don't think you're in the position to threaten Rossano Pagnan. Anyway, please keep in mind that the return of your nephew will require you to give something back to Rossano Pagnan."

"What do you mean?" asked Guo.

"Your activities. It's not worth discussing now. But let's be clear: Pagnan will not give Zhang back to you without something in exchange. He is expecting a certain reciprocity on your part."

"Otherwise?"

"Otherwise we all go back to where we came from, no deal," said Mila.

"So Pagnan will be there in person?"

"Yed, yed, you slant-eyed mudderfucker," Mule managed to mumble.

"What about my nephew?"

"He'll be there too."

"So I'm positive that we'll reach an agreement that gives some advantage to both of us. Ah, Mule, I see that you can almost speak normally again, but your manners have not improved."

"Fuck off."

"See you tomorrow, Mila. Mule, it has been a pleasure."

# 10

Zou Kai smiled.

Tonk looked at him and started slowly shaking his head.

He was beginning to realise that when Zou Kai had suggested they kill themselves, he'd been serious. Deadly serious. The look in his friend's eyes confirmed his fears.

The child, standing still in the doorway of his house, had tears in his eyes, tears that contrasted with the grin on his face. The night air was chilling. The garden looked like an icy wonderland, sculpted by the wind. The dogs were waiting, hungry predators desperate for something to eat. White drool dripped from their ravenous mouths.

"Destroy the Qing to restore the Ming," said Zou Kai. He looked at Tonk one last time. A shadow of fierce resignation crossed his face, a flash of dark lightning that made his intention clearer than a thousand words.

"No!" shouted Tonk. "Zou, don't do it!"

But his friend had made up his mind. He put the .357 Magnum in his mouth and fired.

A dull roar, muffled by the silencer.

A red explosion that destroyed his head.

The smell of burned meat filling the air.

Tonk managed to turn towards the back seat and throw up his fear and his pain.

He didn't think Zou Kai was going to go through with it. But, he realised now, it was well and truly over. This last adventure was the final tragedy of their lives.

They had been through a lot together. They grew up in Wenzou, both cared for by their grandparents after their parents left for Italy. They'd lived a very comfortable life for several years thanks to Mum and Dad sending a monthly allowance far in excess of the average salary of a Chinese factory worker. It was a time of happiness, of joy. After leaving school, though, their parents sent for them to come to Italy. The impact of that new country was immense. They'd ended up in Padua, Tonk working in his parents' min-imarket in Corso del Popolo and Zou Kai in the bar across the road. They worked insane shifts, up to sixteen hours every day.

Little by little they grew up to be men and became friends with others in their circle. Finally they ended up in the Talking Daggers. They pledged allegiance, swore a blood oath and became killers together. They obeyed an inflexible, bloodthirsty master who could use them in whatever way he wanted, force them to do anything, no matter how bad.

And now everything was going to end here, in the garden of this blood-filled villa.

No, they didn't deserve to die like this.

A choked, hysterical scream escaped from his mouth. He started banging his fists on the bulletproof windows of the car. Rage and frustration made him shout meaningless words against the glass, spraying it with his spit.

The dogs howled. Wolves waiting for their pound of flesh. Catching the scent of Zou Kai's blood, they tried to dig their claws into the door of the Seat Leon.

The child called them back.

"Grau, Teufel, come here," he said in a small voice that nonetheless didn't leave room for a reply. "Come on, Daddy will feed you soon," he told the two animals who now looked like tame pets under the caress of his tiny hand. As he spoke, the child sat on a white swing on the grass and the Rottweilers crouched at his feet.

Rossano Pagnan saw immediately that there was something wrong.

There was a silver-grey Mercedes B 190 in front of his gate. It shouldn't have been there.

The Schiavon brothers, his family's bodyguards, were two lifeless lumps of lead-filled beef lying in the garden, left there to rot under the starry sky.

Pagnan couldn't understand it. Or maybe he was afraid he understood it only too well.

The front door was wide open, his eight year-old son on the white swing, a tartan rug around his shoulders, Grau and Teufel wagging their tails at his feet. Giacomo should be in bed at this time. Or at least not in the garden, in the freezing cold, wearing a tartan rug. But there he was, petting the dogs with a strange expression on his face, an expression his father had never seen, one that made him look ten years older.

It looked like an anteater had sneezed a noseful of blood in his wife's Seat Leon. A Chinaman was staring at him from inside, a terrified look in his eyes.

Polenta pulled up in front of the house.

Pagnan jumped out of the car and hurried towards the little fella in his striped shirt and pyjama trousers. A tiny shaman, now running towards him, his arms open, his eyes suddenly full of tears.

"Daddy… Daddy…" he managed to say between the sobs that were shaking his body.

"Don't be afraid, Giacomo. Daddy's here now, don't worry."

"Oh Daddy, Daddy…"

"Giacomo, it's me, what's wrong, baby?" While he tried to console his son, Pagnan felt fear filling his mouth. A shovelful of wet earth binding his words together.

"Mummy…" Giacomo said.

"Mummy, Giacomo, what's wrong with Mummy?" He took the child by the shoulders, kneeling in front of him.

"Mummy's hurt, Daddy! Those men hurt her bad, really bad. I locked them in Mummy's car." He handed Pagnan the key fob.

"You did great, Giacomo. Are you sure Mummy's hurt? Maybe she's only pretending? Where is she?"

"She's inside. I'm fine because I was under the bed."

"That's good, Giacomo. You're a smart boy. Now Daddy's going to go see what's happened.

You stay here with Uncle Polenta. I'll be back soon."

"Hey, young man, how are you? Your dogs are beautiful, you know!" Polenta threw a glance at Pagnan, who nodded in silence and started walking towards the house. Tripe followed him, gun drawn.

For Rossano Pagnan it felt like riding the ghost train at the fun fair. Like a tornado had dropped by to unleash all its violence. His shoes started to creak while he stepped on the thousands of glass fragments all over the marble floor of the main room. His motor magazines were in hundreds of pieces. It looked like they'd been puked up by the bookshelves that had been toppled to the ground. Jackets and suits were torn to shreds and the pieces scattered everywhere, ideograms were painted all over the lavender walls. Of the crystal side table only the frame was left, and the huge cast-iron pendant lightshade had crashed to the floor.

Rossano Pagnan couldn't believe his eyes.

A nauseating stench hit him like a slap. And then he saw her.

His wife's body lay next to the big stone fireplace. Her head had been mashed to a pulp with the poker beside the corpse. Swarms of flies covered her wounds like a vibrating black crust.

Her legs, broken in several places and heavily bruised, were bent at a grotesque angle. Her chest had been opened – actually, literally torn apart – and the butcher who'd done it seemed to have amused himself extracting everything he could find inside: a slow, painstaking job.

Pagnan screamed.

Raging, he launched himself on his wife's body, yelling, desperately trying to swat the flies away.

Tripe, stunned, watched the scene in silence.

When he turned his eyes towards the big leather couch he noticed the body of Rolando, the small Filipino waiter. It had been laid on the cushions so that his head would protrude and his blood drip into a blue plastic bucket placed there on purpose. That's what they'd used to paint the gigantic ideograms on the walls.

The acrid stench that filled the air was the smell of death. Polenta closed his nostrils with one hand. He managed to get to the door, his hand pressed on his mouth, and then threw up an acid jet that stained the outside steps.

Meanwhile, in the main room, Rossano Pagnan was holding his wife's corpse in his arms, cradling it.

"My wife…" he whispered. "*My* fucking wife."

He wasn't able to say anything else.

• • •

"Fuck. We might as well have kissed his ass while we were at it!"

"You'd have liked that, wouldn't you?"

Mule hated that tone of voice. Especially coming from the mouth of some kid with red dreadlocks who'd had the temerity to interrupt a pleasant meet-up with Pagnan and the whole gang so she could pass judgment on what they should do and how they should do it.

"Fucking hell, you ever going to stop trying to provoke me?"

"Hey, chill, man! I didn't start it."

"Fuck you, I've been busting my balls for years for Mr Pagnan, I work like an idiot, get hold of that fucking traitor who the boss had practically treated like a son, one of our guys gets killed for his troubles and not only does the boss fail to thank us, he tells us all to get to fuck. And who does he trust in the end? A woman. And a total stranger at that."

"This drives you crazy, right?"

"Of course it drives me crazy, for fuck's sake!"

"Because I'm a woman…"

"*Especially* because you're a woman!"

"…and because I'm smarter than you."

"Christ! I really need to teach you a lesson."

"So, come on! What are you waiting for? I'll park and you can teach me that goddamned lesson. Since I met you, it's been nothing but talk, talk, talk. The only action I've seen from you is taking a punch from a Chinaman."

"Fuck it! Stop! I've fucking had enough!"

"Oh, finally! Took your time, didn't you?"

"Stop the car!"

"Whatever you say."

They were speeding towards Mila's home. The road to Arsego. They'd driven past Vigodarzere and were close to Saletto. As soon as she saw a space, Mila slowed down and parked the car. She opened the door and got out.

Mule looked at her, dumbfounded.

"Come on, Big Man, get out. Don't make me wait."

"Oh for fuck's sake," he said huffing.

Mila had reached the uneven ground of the frozen field next to the roadside. Two feeble streetlamps lit the surrounding area. She was waiting for him.

Mule realised that there were no tricks, the girl was preparing for a dust-up with him. That was it.

"How long do I have to wait?"

She was driving him completely mental.

"So you really want me to knock the living daylights out of you!"

"You wish!"

He looked at her, surprised by her insistence and furious at the way she was treating him. He got out of the car and reached her as she was donning a pair of specs with yellow lenses.

"What's up, you have eye problems?"

"What do you think?"

"Mm, you're really pissing me off!"

"I hope so."

"You know, I don't think I can beat up a woman."

"Bollocks," she said. "But if that's what's holding you up, I can help you out there."

Mila smiled. It looked like she couldn't wait to get started. An eager child. She drew closer and punched him straight in the face.

Mule felt something crack inside his nose. Then nothing for a second, and suddenly a terrible pain gripped him. Blood flowed copiously into his mouth, which was still swollen from the Chinaman's fist.

"You dirty fucking bitch. Now you're really pissing me off!"

"So you said. What're you going to do about it?"

He attacked her like a wounded animal. First he tried a right uppercut that Mila avoided easily, then a straight left that also missed.

"What are you doing? Some kind of dance, is

it?" Mila taunted him, staring at him as if she already knew precisely what moves he was about to make.

She kept moving on her feet, elegant and lethal. She swayed like a reed under the moonlit cloak of a night sky patterned with pale stars.

It was so cold it was hard to breathe.

Mule charged again. He feinted once, twice, shot a left hook that Mila parried with her forearm, followed immediately by a right jab. Mila dodged it, took two steps forward and whacked him with her right hand, a chop to the back of the head, then pivoted on her left leg and delivered a roundhouse kick that struck him in the pit of the stomach.

*Thump!*

Breathlessness.

Mule was hurting. Mila had been so fast he hadn't seen where the kick had come from. He found himself grasping at thin air. Then, with the last of his strength, he threw himself forward with all his weight, trying to knock the woman over. This time he hit her torso in a clumsy tackle, leading with his head, like a bull.

But Mila was waiting for him and managed to slide on her side to cushion the blow. They fell together. With a quick twist she ended up on top of him and hit him in the ribs: a series of fast, effective punches intended to weaken him, so she could pick him apart at her leisure.

She wasn't in a hurry and didn't want to hurt him too badly, just enough to prove which of them was capable of beating up the other. Clear and simple.

Her specs were still where they were supposed to be; they hadn't fallen off during the fight. So she'd been able to film the whole scene. It might be useful at some point.

Mule had crouched under her hail of blows, practically in the foetal position, protecting his ribs with his arms as best he could. He tried to kick her but the Fury was straddling him, beating the living crap out of him.

Suddenly he felt her releasing him. He took the chance to get back on his feet, limping and groggy.

Mila was staring at him, still moving on her feet. A predator, a perfect warrior who came back to life with each fight, each brawl, every move rehearsed over and over again, thousands of times. It was a nice feeling. To feel so fluid, dynamic, quick. To smell the blood of the enemy.

Mule was light years away from feeling anything like that. He stood there, motionless, his face purple and the front of his white shirt, where Mila had punched him over and over again, red with blood.

"Come on, let's go again," that fire-haired demon said to him.

Fuck right off, he thought. He'd had enough. He was a man of common sense and, behind his alpha-male attitude, he was perfectly able to recognise when a situation was only going to deteriorate. Mule wasn't thick. You didn't become Pagnan's right-hand man by being stupid.

Sure that girl could scrap a bit. But sooner or later there would be an opportunity to teach her a proper lesson. He just needed to wait. He settled for giving her a sideways glare.

"Let's forget about it," he said. "Maybe next time we'll see how good you are with a gun. No more of this karate shit."

"Whatever, honey-bun."

What was one more jibe. Mule climbed back into the car, just in time to hear his phone ring.

It was Polenta, who informed him of the massacre in the boss' home and didn't spare the details, however disturbing.

"You need to come over straight away. The boss is devastated. He just wants you. And Mila of course."

"On our way," replied Mule.

Great, he thought a second later. The girl's going to be right next to me the whole time.

"Good, we're waiting. And make sure she gets

here. If she gives you any crap, sort it out. Do what you must. No pissing about, OK?"

"Don't worry," said Mule.

Meanwhile, Mila had started the car.

"Trouble?" she asked.

"Yes, big time. Carnage at Pagnan's villa. The Chinks took advantage of the fact that we'd let our guard down and struck while we were all busy messing around like fucking idiots with Longhin. That asshole has been an absolute disaster, worse than the plague."

"Shit happens."

"I hope Pretty Boy is having fun with him."

"I imagine so."

"Listen…"

"Yes?"

"We need to go to Pagnan's straight away and update him on the agreement we reached with Guo. I don't know if he'll still be OK to meet up with that Chinese son of a bitch, but we need to have a watertight plan. Tomorrow we have to blow the fuckers away. Whatever the cost."

"Arranging the meeting at the farmhouse is the best idea. I think it's the perfect place for an ambush. If I'm not wrong, there's an old furnace around there."

"Yes, about five hundred metres away."

"Awesome! No problem."

"What do you mean, 'no problem'?" mumbled an irritated Mule.

"I mean no problem. I mean, I'll be on top of the furnace with a sniper's rifle. And with the right telemetry, I'll knock them down one by one."

"So you said. Who do you think you are? Rambo's daughter?"

"Nice. You just quoted John Ashton in *Beverly Hills Cop II*. But anyway. Trust me, this is the best way. They'll be caught in the middle. You guys shooting at them from the front and me mowing them down while they try to run. Thing is, I need a spotter."

"A what?"

"Damn it, you people know jack shit about military techniques!"

"No, you're right. Say that word again?"

"Spotter."

"OK, I did hear correctly. What the fuck do you mean?"

"Hmm… OK, let's see: you know what a sniper is?"

"Of course… someone who can shoot from a distance. And hit the target."

"Great, at least you have a bit of a clue. A spotter is someone who works alongside the sniper. He's in charge of covering fire, helps identify the target and adjust the sniper's aim, carries most of the equipment. Sniper and spotter are a cell working on the total annihilation of their enemy, one man at the time. It's evident you won't be able to manage the sight adjustments, but at least you'll be able to help identify the targets with a pair of binoculars and carry some of the equipment, right?"

"Christ, yes, you can bet on it!"

"If your boss agrees, of course."

"And you seriously think you'll be able to pick off all the Chinese one at a time, including that dirty bastard Guo?"

"Well, that's the idea."

"Pagnan will be delighted."

"Great. Now, a question: where exactly are we going?"

"The hills. Towards Muson. That's where Pagnan lives."

"Cool. We'll be there in fifteen minutes. Hold tight."

Mila put the pedal to the metal, the Focus darted away. A blue shadow in the winter night. She already knew where Pagnan lived, of course, but she hadn't imagined she'd be walking in through the front door.

# 11

*From Mila Zago's journal:*

So, Dr Berton, how's the reading
experience going?

Yes, I know, I haven't told you anything
about what happened recently but hey,
bear with me. I need to be able to explain
my actions. Pretend that my journal is like
one of those boring memoirs written by
some old fart of a lawyer who's mastered
the art of long-windedness. Come on, just
a few minutes more and I'll get to the
point, promise. You can trust me. I am
pretty sure that what I'm writing is more

interesting than the average application to dismiss. Am I right or what?

OK, where was I...?

I had sworn to myself that I would go after Pagnan until the bitter end. And as my project grew, I felt an uncontrollable rage grow too. At that point, I didn't know how I'd do it, but I had a pretty good idea how it was all going to end.

It was as if the combination of my mother abandoning me, my father being murdered, and the rape had resulted in completely removing the concept of forgiveness from me.

After my father's death, I wanted to see all those involved crawling at my feet. Dark, agonising nightmares inhabited my sleep every night. I fantasised that I could crush my enemies, destroy their faces by crushing them under my feet.

My love for my grandparents kept me alive, but it also fed my thirst for revenge. Through the constant training he made me undergo, my grandfather was – more or less consciously – pushing me to the limit, helping me to develop the killer instinct that was ripening like a poisonous fruit. Every hour-long run, every shot fired at the range, every bruise on my skin was a small step towards the death of Pagnan and his men.

Then, a few years later, my grandparents passed as well. They shrivelled up like leaves in autumn. They went together. Suddenly. One night they closed their eyes forever, in bed, holding each other's hand.

They left a tin box containing various bits and pieces for me: some coloured candles to remember them by on starry nights; the old mushroom guidebook I had leafed through so many times in preparation for our forays into the woods; Grandma's necklace, a silver coin with a hole in the centre with a leather strap; the Hohner chromatic mouth organ with a bullet stuck to the right hand side, the bullet that had saved Grandpa's life on the Austrian front; a piece of wrapping paper on which he had jotted down the name, address and other details of a brother in arms with whom he had kept in touch after the war and who was working on a top-secret project that, according to him, would be of great interest to me in days to come.

No point telling you more: I think that

secret projects should stay secret.

The demise of my family was a key moment in my life.

The peace that their sweet deaths gave me triggered a new consciousness. Now nobody would know or judge what I did.

I started working on my grand plan with a newfound passion. I got a lucrative job as a fashion model for an important leather shop. Thanks to my slender physique I soon became very much in demand amongst the ateliers of the Padua province. With my inheritance and what I was earning with my job, I renovated my grandparents' home and bought a small piece of land in the Seven Communities plateau, where I could hone my skills in private.

Usually I drive there in an old, metal-red Subaru Forester. Just like I did today. I cross the Valsugana and head up: the hairpins, the smell of genuine Asiago cheese from the cheesemakers along the route, the cowsheds with their animals snorting and grunting. Then, further along, I see the ski tows in the grass and, higher up, the small houses studding a sea of green that in winter is covered by a thick,

white, solid coating which cross-country
skiers slide along in silence.

Once I get to the plateau I drive up a dirt
road climbing through the meadows and
into the wood. Then, after several miles,
finally, in total seclusion, it appears – the
big house, built from strong, sturdy Scots
pine, beautiful in its old-fashioned
simplicity.

The shooting range is not enough for me
any longer.

I need to be able to practice with all the
weapons I want, alone, where I grew up.

So today I am in the woods again.

And I have something nice to play with.

Armalite AR 15 assault rifle, thirty
rounds magazine, Zeiss dioptric riflescope,
5.56mm bullets. Semi-automatic shot
selector.

When it impacts, a 5.56mm bores a
small, neat, clean, flawless hole. If you
know how to use it, a rifle like this is
lethal. I have some experience.

The target placed on the fir in front of
me is soon riddled with holes. Bark and
wood splinters fly everywhere under the
hail of bullets. My ear protection saves my
hearing, the recoil is minimal and

somehow pleasantly massages my shoulder.

Then I change weapons.

A Colt .45. A classic.

Seven bullets in the magazine and one in the chamber: half the capacity of modern guns, but we're talking eight hollow point .45 bullets, double the impact and half the recoil of a .9mm. An advantage that makes all the difference. In some situations, survival is in the details.

Thus engaged, I forget what I am becoming.

Resin, gun smoke that fills up the deep, musky smell of the wood, the air chewed apart by the shots. A delicious cocktail I can't live without.

I am a junkie.

For violence.

Let's be honest. To walk around knowing I'm a lethal weapon is an amazing feeling. I suspect it happens to you as well. Yes, I know, you're thinking that I'm still writing about myself, drawing unlikely comparisons because I'm paranoid. Maybe. Sure, you're not a traditional kind of weapon, but in a way you're more of one than I am: your profession allows you to decide who's guilty and who isn't. Yes, indeed, that's usually the role of a judge. But what about dismissals? And summary trials, committals? Yes, you're right, you only apply the law, but still you've a tonne of power in your hands, no shit.

So I expect you know perfectly well the feeling of walking around knowing you're a weapon.

I haven't forgiven my mother and I haven't accepted yet that my father was killed.

I'd like to have him here to tell him how much I miss him. To show him how strong I have become.

But when the last bullet tunnels into the bark of the tree and the noise of the shot disappears like the promise of death tossed into the air, he's not there, and the woods are watching me.

They are watching me with the eyes of a doe, appearing on the edge of a clearing with her fawn.

They don't judge me.

They look at me in a tender way, or at least so it seems while I walk amongst the blueberry bushes, their greens and blues breaking up the yellow gold of the

chanterelles that have sprouted after the
last rain of the summer.
    I smile.
    I greet that mother with her child.
    I pick up my weapons.
    I fill up my bag again and go back home.

# 12

Dark clouds draped the sky, a black blanket you could get lost in.

Rossano Pagnan lit a Marlboro and stared in silence at the freshly turned soil in his garden. He had just finished burying Marisa's remains.

His wife had been torn to pieces because he wasn't there.

The fact itself was little more than a nuisance to him – he had long since ceased any form of intimacy with her.

But it had all ended in such a pitiful way. They'd been ignoring each other for years, while she squandered the money he managed to set aside with his business activities. That was it. All there was to them being man and wife. Still, their life together had been different once.

He sighed. Tiredness was wearing him out. The war against the Chinaman was turning into full-scale annihilation, and he wasn't the one who started it.

His mobile rung.

"Boss, you there?"

"Of course I'm here, Pretty Boy. Who do you think picked up the phone?"

"Sorry. I heard what happened. Bastards!"

"Bastards is too nice for them, for fuck's sake."

"True. I just wanted to say that I'm done with Longhin. He drowned in his own blood. The Newbie is cleaning up the mess I made in the bowling lane. I'll chop the corpse to pieces, throw it in the meat grinder and prepare some first-rate mince."

"*Bueno*."

"You talk like Tex Willer, boss."

Pagnan smiled. He loved the Tex Willer Wild West comic books. Each time he read one it felt like he was meeting an old friend. Predictable, comfortable. Full of stereotypes, but suitably manly.

"I wish," said Pagnan. "I'd have killed all the bad guys by now. Instead, we're still some distance from ending this."

"That's true, boss, and it's not good."

"Who's your favourite amongst the Tex Willer characters?"

"My favourite?" asked Pretty Boy, who was not expecting such a question at that moment, especially so suddenly. But he replied without hesitation. "Tiger Jack." Tex Willer's Native American friend.

"Oh. Why's that?"

"Actually I don't know, I always had a soft spot for the Redskins, the idea, you know – loyalty, long hair, nature, riding bareback, all that shit."

"Right, all that shit."

"Right."

"Listen, Pretty Boy."

"Yes, boss?"

"They have to pay for this."

"You can bet on it."

"Chop Longhin up and come here as soon as you're done."

"Count on it."

"While I'm waiting, I'll feed the dogs. Got a new diet I want to try out."

"What's that?"

"Chinamen. One dead, one alive."

"Fuck!"

"Can't wait to hear the cries of the one who's still alive."

"Sure you will. His screams will be heard a hundred miles away, in Parma."

"See you later."

"Ladies and gentlemen, please allow me to say a couple of words about Rottweiler Metzgerhund."

Rossano Pagnan's face bore a steady, sneering look. They'd just killed his wife and he was commencing a speech that promised to be a tad soporific.

"Rottweil is a town on the Neckar river, where this type of dog was utilised to guard the butchers' meat."

After all the dismay and rage, anticipating a first small taste of revenge allowed Pagnan to resurrect some of the panache he used to have in his best days.

Mila was getting ready to witness a collective ritual of violence, the second in only a few hours, and was starting to think she might end up losing control of the situation. After all it had been she who had initiated this escalation of cruelty by suggesting Guo strike at Pagnan while he was defenceless, but she hadn't expected such a sickening cycle of violence. She hadn't thought Pagnan would end up feeding a man to his dogs – alive. It was too much, even for her. She was seriously considering killing them all here and now, and fucking off.

Sure, they would do a pretty good job of slaughtering each other, and that was precisely what she was after. But she wanted both bosses: Rossano Pagnan and Guo Xiaoping. And the only way to catch them together was to survive until 5 in the afternoon the following day and see her plan to completion.

So she decided to wait.


A short line led by Pagnan with Mila following him and then Mule and Tripe dragging the two Chinamen – one dead, one alive – by the arms. They'd taken them out of the car and were walking towards what looked like an enclosed dog-training area.

They were nearly there when something unexpected happened.

A scream.

An instant later, Tripe was cupping his testicles and rolling on the ground as if he had been bitten by a tarantula. Tonk, who until then seemed to be ready to slip silently into the next world, was aiming a gun as big as a cannon at Mule's head.

"I'll shoot him! I'll shoot him, you bastards!" he was shouting, out of his mind and possessed by a homicidal rage.

He had moved so fast he'd blindsided

everybody. Pagnan went pale, but a second later he put a hand in his trouser pocket, fished out a nail file and started to smooth off his thumbnail.

"Whatever you like," he said.

Tonk wasn't expecting that response. While his face tangled itself up in a mask of disbelief, Mila took the chance to dive to one side and open fire with a .45 she'd quickly drawn from its holster.

*Chunk! Chunk!*

Double impact. Lethal.

Two red holes opened simultaneously in Tonk's forehead. Mila completed her somersault on the frozen ground of the garden and got straight back on her feet. Just in time to see the Chinaman's legs give way and he crumpled to the ground clutching the gun he'd snatched from Tripe, as if it was a crucifix given to him by the priest administering the final rites.

"Astonishing," Pagnan said. "I would like to have recorded that."

"Thank you," Mule commented dryly, unleashing all his rage against Pagnan. "If it was up to you, this asshole could have killed me no problem, right?"

"Don't get upset, Mule. It was only a distraction to allow Mila to do what she did. Right, Mila?"

"I'd have managed regardless. Still, the nail file was pretty cool."

"See?" gloated Pagnan. "Tripe, stuff the Chinamen in the coldroom off the garage, and while you're at it, stick the Schiavon brothers in there as well. We've no time for more burials now. We're going upstairs to the attic to discuss the details of tomorrow's meeting. When you're done, join us there. Understood?"

"Perfectly, boss."

The enormous loft room was the trashiest thing Mila had ever seen.

The walls were covered in heavily stained red drapes, the smell of stale beer made the air heavy, the marble floor peeked out here and there from under a series of rugs of various different colours, piled randomly on top of one another and adorned with a series of greasy stains that matched those on the walls.

In the centre of the room was an ebony table with mother-of-pearl inlays covered in an impressive number of empty beer bottles and knocked-over tumblers and a silver chandelier, its five branches drowned in wax.

In one corner of the room an old, acid green fringed sofa was in its death throes. In front of it, a velvet armchair that had probably once been pink but was now too pale and faded to tell for sure. Scattered about the room, there was a mess of upturned lamps, strange little blonde-wood boxes, covered in arcane symbols similar to swastikas, that were brimming with silver necklaces, rolled-up carpets, silk pyjamas, various junk of mysterious origin. In each of the four corners, a bookshelf stuffed with adventure books and comics – the white spines with the blue title that characterised Tex Willer next to the black volumes of Dylan Dog, the horror series.

"I love India, Tex and adventure," said Pagnan theatrically, for no specific reason.

Mule, still aching from the beating up he had received, grunted.

"Please make yourselves comfortable on the couch. Anything to drink?"

"Yes please," said Mila, and added: "I love Tex Willer and his friends too. I'll have a Nardini grappa, straight."

"Great!" said Pagnan. "Finally a woman who's not all snooty about what she drinks. What about you, Mule?"

Mule grimaced. "I'll have a Nardini as well."

"So," said the boss, his face growing serious. "I have some questions for the two of you. But let's start from the beginning. How did it go with that son of a bitch, Guo?"

"Well, we managed to get him to agree to the meeting," said Mule. "Honestly, I'd hoped that asshole would have been a little more impressed at seeing the severed heads. But he didn't even blink. Not only that, but he told us this unbelievably long story about the Chinese mafia. Fuck, it felt like being back in school. In the front row."

Mila didn't speak.

"He didn't even flinch, you say?"

"Didn't raise an eyebrow. That old bastard has steel for nerves."

"OK, but at least we secured the meeting at the old farmhouse, right?"

"Five o'clock this afternoon," said Mila.

"Good. By the way, Mule, how did you get those marks on your face? Did you exchange words with Mike Tyson?"

"I said something that fucking Chink didn't like. He got two of his men to beat me up."

"Fuck him. He plays the hard man with my men, that's one more thing he'll have to pay for."

Mila kept silent. She emptied her glass in one gulp and poured more grappa for herself. She didn't want to cause further harm to the wounded pride of Pagnan's right-hand man; also, his lie might end up working in her favour. Avoiding mention of the fisticuffs out in the field had certain advantages. Making Pagnan believe that Mule could keep her under control wasn't a bad thing.

"So, how are we going to do it, Mila?"

"How are we going to do what?"

"This evening's little party, what's the plan?"

"I bring my supergun and kill all the bad guys. Just like in the comics."

"I need more than that. Don't think you'll get out of here until you've explained it to me in detail." Pagnan scratched his belly and poured a second glass of grappa.

"No problem. Although I don't think I'd have any trouble getting out of here if I wanted to."

"Oi!"

"Anyway, my plan is to use the old furnace."

"How? It's too far from the farmhouse."

"I thought I'd already explained."

"Tell me again."

"Well, with a normal rifle it wouldn't be possible. But with an M501 Beretta there's no problem. Piece of piss for a sharpshooter like me."

This time Pagnan's eyes lit up in genuine surprise.

"Shit, Mule, are you hearing this chick?"

"I'm hearing."

"Suppose I'm buying. Let's assume you have such a rifle and you can hit your target from that distance. I don't want to know how you learned how to shoot, I've got it, you're better than Billy the Kid. But I wonder, do you really think I trust what you're telling me? I mean, what would prevent you from shooting everybody, including my own men?"

"Nothing. Maybe I will. Point is, you have no choice. I'll tell you a bit more. And then if you don't want me to do anything, I won't. But you'll be back where you started."

"Good. But I'll tell you this for starters: Mule's going to climb onto the roof of the furnace with you and he'll blow your head off as soon as you do something wrong. He'll be all over you like a rash, close as a tattoo on your sweet ass."

"Great," said Mule. "I actually hope that this bullshitting bitch messes up so I'll finally be able to fill her pretty little red head with lead."

"I'm terrified," replied Mila promptly.

"You should be," confirmed Pagnan.

"Allow me to remind you of the two million euros that were in your accountants' bags and that are now in a safe place that I know the location of – and you don't."

"I haven't forgotten. That's why you're still alive."

"As you like. You're talking like the bad guy in a decidedly mediocre police movie, you know. Anyway, as I said, it's not going to be a problem. Mule and I get there early, find a nice spot. Then you get there with your people. Then the Chinese come. They don't know I'll be shooting at them. As soon as they get out of their cars you start welcoming them with all the gracious words you can think of, and as soon as you're done I start picking them off one by one. When we're done, we'll figure out my new role in Padua's criminal underworld."

"What do you mean?"

"I hope you don't think I'm cleaning up your mess because I'm a Good Samaritan. Let's be clear about this. If I help you with the Chinese, here's what's going to happen next: we split the money fifty-fifty – the two million, I mean – and I get thirty per cent of everything you earn through your businesses. Prostitution, drugs, toxic waste, illegal betting, I want a third of it all. And I want to manage it, along with yourself, of course."

"Hey, are you high on something?"

"Not at all, old man. Why the fuck do you think I'm helping you? I'll say it one last time. First, because you're the goose that lays the golden eggs. Second, because you're a local and I don't want these Chinese here in my homeland. Third, because I want to be the first woman to lead a criminal organisation. Jointly, at least. The world is changing. Try to see it as a creative way of balancing out the gender quotas. Are you up for it?" She looked at him.

"You're really quite demanding. How about this: once we're done with the China connection we sit down and…"

"No deal, Daddy-O. We're already sitting down and I won't accept any conditions. If you don't agree, we can just drop it and I'll go home. With the two million."

"For fuck's sake, you're a greedy little viper," Mule said.

"Nice comparison, but that's not the point. Your real issue here is that you're unable to get out of the mess you're in on your own. You might not want to admit it, but you know I'm your only hope."

"Mila, don't let things go to your head! How do you think I created all this? Do you really think you can treat me like some snotty-nosed kid?" Pagnan was smiling, but his eyes were full of fire.

"No, we misunderstand each other. I don't want to pull the rug from under you. In exchange for a share of the pie, I just want to help you squeeze a city like Padua – and let's not forget the surrounding province. It's juicy, like a fat apple, a Granny Smith. It's not enough to take a bite here and there like you do. I want to take it all. Mind, I'm not saying you're ineffective, I respect the network you've established, nothing to say about that. But allow me to say that you could benefit from the assistance of someone more modern, more aggressive. Your methods were great twenty years ago. Since then Padua has changed, and you and yours seem to have been left a little behind."

"Listen to me, girlie: I'll pretend I didn't hear you. For your own good. Yes, I've seen what you can do. But don't think you can frighten me just because you carved up a couple of Chinese fuckheads, you understand me?" Pagnan's voice had turned into a dull hiss.

"Pagnan, I'm not saying you're scared." Mila was smiling, amused. "All I'm saying is that at the moment you're in deep shit and you don't know how to get out of it, while I can get you out of all of it – clean. If I mention spotters or an M501 Beretta to you and your men you don't even know what I'm talking about. That's bad, really bad. Guo is the leader of a local organisation he founded, the Talking Daggers. But he's also the White Paper Fan of 14K, a Chinese Triad that's branching out throughout the north-east. It would be better to remove the blister before it bursts, do you understand? This is a new type of war for you, for Mule, for Polenta, for all of you. You can't win it the old way. You need to step up. I *am* your step up. And I'm available. If you want to, grab the chance. Otherwise, you're on your own."

Pagnan rubbed his eyes with his index fingers. He started to feel tired. Remained silent for a good ten seconds.

"And if I say no, you'll go to Guo?"

"Who knows. After all, I'm holding his nephew hostage, and you have fuck all."

"Right. My stupid pride."

"Come on, don't start to buckle now," Mila comforted him.

"If I give you what you ask for, will you promise to work with me?"

"Cross my heart."

# 13

A pass from Tuzzolino splits the defence in half.

Double step forward, John Parco lifts his stick up to his shoulder and releases a slap shot. Low to high. Right to left.

The puck enters the upper corner of Paolo Della Bella's goal.

Three.

The fans are delirious.

Hodegart. The Asiago hockey stadium.

Ice hockey playoffs, game one: the Asiago Lions against the Milan Vipers.

We lead three-nil.

I love watching the guys play by instinct, scoring one goal after another against the usual opponents, the ones who ordinarily defeat us.

I love Veneto, I love my land. Write that in your folder, Dr Berton. Many people didn't even know that the Seven Communities plateau existed until the mayor and townsfolk of Asiago asked for a referendum on whether they should be annexed to Trentino Alto Adige. And the result was a "no"!

9.30pm. I'm sitting on the stands with a Benetton ski overall, Asolo hiking boots with Vibram soles, a red and yellow scarf proudly displaying a lion's mane; I'm here to support the Asiago Ice Hockey guys.

Every time I go up to Enego to train and breathe the clean air I come here on Saturday evenings. With a plastic cup full of mulled wine to warm me up in the cold air of the Hodegart, I shout along with the two thousand other supporters until I'm hoarse. I watch the boys darting along on the thin ice, scrapping once again with their fiercest rivals, the Milan Vipers. North east against north west. A healthy sporting rivalry.

Hockey makes me go hog wild. Because it's the perfect end to an evening. An unexpected dessert prepared with natural ingredients, all good stuff from the plateau.

Add this to your folder as well, Dr Berton.

I drink in the adrenaline rush that Parco's goal gives me.

As faces turn progressively redder and the hot VOV and brandy cocktails flow down the fans' throats, as Strazzabosco is sent off for tripping an opposition forward and the red-and-yellow spectators explode in a surprised, frustrated "Ooh" replete with blasphemies and the customary insulting of the referee, I settle down in the cold of the Hodegart and think about my plans. And once again I repeat to myself that it's the right thing to do.

I just bought the specs. Face-hugging, built-in video camera, yellow Polaroid corrective lenses, 20 gigabyte memory, 640x480 resolution, USB connection to download the .mpeg movies.

I can shoot movies from my perspective, and there's a ten-hour battery life. Unbelievable.

When I'm done recording what I'm interested in, I'll edit it all into a single file.

Maybe you're wondering why. Are you, Dr Berton? I don't think you really need to know.

Let's put it like this: I'm on the side of the good guys and I'm going to kick the bad guys' asses in a way they'll understand. An eye for an eye, sister. End of story.

It is a little like playing hockey. There are rules. But here everybody needs to stick to them. Not like in the Italian law courts.

The rules of my game say that if you shoot, I shoot; if you kill, I kill; if you inflict a wound, I inflict a wound; if you cross the line, I remember. My memory doesn't have an expiration date.

Are you following, Doctor?

Are you aware that the inquiry you're leading will end up nowhere?

Anyway, if you still believe in judicial process and the legal system, good for you. I quit.

And you can't prevent me from doing it my way. Sure, you can try to catch me, if you want. But you won't. Believe me. You don't know who I am. Yet. Still, let me give

you a suggestion. Take a half day from time
to time and come to Hodegart.

Now I'll return to the game. I want to
see how many we'll score in the second
half. Promise me that sooner or later you'll
come watch a game.

Or whatever.

Keep safe. Speak to you soon.

Yours,


Mila

# 14

The road before her was a dark snake crossing a terrain hardened by winter frost. Sparse blades of grass dotted the fields; the rays of a huge orange sun, still high above the horizon, cast iridescent reflections onto the canvas of a cold, blue sky.

Mila was inspecting the plains from the top of the old abandoned furnace. A shelter made of irregular bricks in the middle of nowhere. An enormous dinosaur of a thing, perforated by tunnels and old combustion chambers. On two sides, a huge smokestack, a guard of honour, like the antennae of an insect.

About six hundred yards away, directly in front

of her, Pagnan's old farmhouse squatted like a block of stone.

Standing next to her Mule was looking towards it, shaking his head in disbelief.

They had just climbed a crumbling staircase with two heavy tennis bags full of weapons and other bits and bobs, risking falling and breaking their necks.

The Ford Focus was parked next to the wall furthest away from the road, a green tarpaulin draped over it.

Mila shouldered her M501 Beretta. The perfectly shaped muscles in her back rippled under her black spandex halter-top as she placed the rifle on its cradle. With dextrous fingers, she mounted the Zeiss Diavari ZA zoom lens.

Mule kept staring at her with an expression that showed his discomfort. He broke the silence with what sounded like an admission of guilt.

"Mila, I don't think I can help you."

"I'm not surprised. Don't worry, I wasn't counting on you. It'll be more than enough if you can just shut up. It's not too far. It'll be like shooting clay pigeons."

"This doesn't mean I won't keep an eye on you."

"Whatever you like," replied Mila. She masked her hatred of him with a yawn.

Mule raised his hip flask of whisky to his lips. He couldn't understand how Mila could wear nothing but a vest. It was damned chilly.

"Aren't you cold, dressed like that?"

"Cold is a state of mind," replied Mila.

"Fancy a sip?" he asked pointing at his flask.

"No, thanks."

"It's a Lagavulin, you know. Single malt, very peaty; the drink of connoisseurs. It'll warm you up like hell."

"I don't want to mess with my balance at the moment. I need to focus, and that's not going to be easy if you keep on talking bullshit. Please, shut up."

"What else is in your bag?" he asked.

"Wait and see."

Mule grinned. He waited. Looked out from the roof of the abandoned furnace where they loomed over the landscape like vultures waiting for corpses to tuck into.

It was 3pm. Exactly.


The black BMW Series 5 drove past the furnace and parked in front of the farmhouse.

Pagnan got out of the car, dressed in black. He had slept like a baby; he felt he deserved it after the discussion with Mila and Mule that carried on until dawn. He was wearing a pair of Ray-Ban

Wayfarers. Someone had told him they were back in fashion, although he'd forgotten who.

Pretty Boy sprang out from the driving seat, his long jet-black hair waving in the wind and wearing the usual outfit: hiking boots, jeans, a blood-stained vest and the ever-dependable blue apron that made him look like a cowherd from South Tirol. Pretty Boy never changed his clothes.

As soon as his extremely expensive shoes touched the ground, Pagnan dug his phone out of his pocket. He dialled while Polenta, Tripe and the Newbie, all in black as well, wriggled out from the car and walked towards the farmhouse.

Mule picked up after two rings.

"Are you there?"

"We're all set."

"Well done. Let me talk to Mila."

"OK."

"All under control, Mila?"

"I have you perfectly framed in my zoom lens. If I squeeze the trigger now, you're dead meat."

Pagnan gave her the finger.

"Can you see this?" he said.

"Well enough for you to lose it in a couple of seconds."

"Hee hee!"

"Right, hee hee."

"What's Mule doing?"

"He's holding a Desert Eagle in his right hand and aiming it at my head. I hope he doesn't fire it. I'd die but he'd be deaf for the rest of his life."

"OK. Well, don't fuck up. Kill the Chinese on my signal."

"What's the signal?"

"Guo getting out of his car. I don't give a fuck about the others. They can dance the twist for all I care. OK?"

"OK, old man. Take it easy."

"Don't call me old man."

"OK, old man."

"Fine, let's stop this right here. Let me talk to Mule."

"Here he is."

"Mule, can you hear me?"

"Loud and clear."

"Good. Keep an eye on her."

"You bet, boss."

"I'll see you at the farmhouse once it's all over."

Pagnan ended the call.

His men dragged Zhang Wen out of the car by his arms and legs. Where his hands had been severed, he was still wearing the bandages Mila had put on. They'd gone red but the laces she'd fastened around his armpits had prevented him from dying of blood loss.

The sight of his corpse-like face was quite

something. Emaciated, sunken by pain and hunger, a macabre mask foreshadowing death, the grim reaper ready to welcome him. Trash, hanging from his torturers' hands. An exhausted, tormented scarecrow figure. Pagnan's men placed a thick rope around his neck, the other end secured to one of the posts in the wooden fence surrounding the farmhouse.

The chill hit his skin and made him shiver. He didn't seem human anymore. Pagnan looked at him, satisfied, scratched his ball-sack and spat on the ground.

Meanwhile Pretty Boy and the Newbie had gone into the house and opened one or two of the ground floor windows.

With Polenta and Tripe standing behind him like reprobate guardian angels, Pagnan studied the clear sky and the uncultivated field in front of him. He assumed what he felt was a tough-guy stance and kept staring towards the horizon.

He was lost in contemplation of that distant vista when his phone started buzzing, persistently. Considering the timing, "bad" didn't describe the half of it. That sound was a real irritation. Still, bad timing or not, he decided to pick up. Maybe some small talk would help ease the mounting tension, take his mind off things.

As soon as he recognised the number he

regretted accepting the call. But he'd already pressed the button. Too late.

"Mr Pagnan?" A thin, high-pitched voice, like an annoying, tiresome child's. More importantly, it wasn't Benny Marcato's voice, even though his name had appeared on the mobile's display.

"Sorry, but... who are you?" replied Pagnan, rankled by the surprise.

"I'm Dr Livia Baldan, calling on behalf of the Mayor of Muson. I'm contacting you in order to–"

"I got it!" roared Pagnan. "I've already agreed everything concerning the riding stables with the Mayor. Everything's all set, his damned speech is safe as houses, what else do you want?"

"I wanted to make sure that–"

"Well, you made sure," said Pagnan in a tone of voice that didn't brook a reply.

"I apologise, I didn't mean to bother you."

"Apologies aren't enough, Dr Baldan. I'm here dealing with an issue that's been keeping me awake nights and you call me on my mobile about some triviality. Are you taking the piss? I already talked with the Mayor, like I said, so coordinate with him and leave me alone, or I'll get downright abusive."

"OK, OK, don't get annoyed, Mr Pagnan."

"Don't get annoyed? What the fuck are you on? Of course I'm going to get annoyed, you stupid asshole. I'm standing here talking to you while I should be focussed on solving a problem the size of Prato della Valle. And that's the biggest square in Europe, for your information. So stop fucking with my concentration!"

Silence.

"Have a nice day!" and, without saying anything else, he cut the connection.

This was his land; nobody could tell him what to do here. Deep in thought once again, he spotted the dark shapes of two cars at the bottom of the road. He took out a packet of Marlboro from the inside pocket of his jacket. He lifted it to his mouth and extracted one with his lips.

He narrowed his eyes to combat the sun's glare. The cars were getting bigger as they drove along the dirt road.

He breathed blue-coloured smoke towards them.

He added his scorn to it.

"Very good," said Guo, satisfied with how things were going. After a lot of hurdles, everything was finally getting easier. It was a matter of keeping the faith.

He was on the phone with Arturo Lasalandra, the president of the provincial SME confederation, fine-tuning the details of his speech at the round table on cultural integration.

"Mr Guo, please allow me to congratulate you on the meticulousness of your speech. We'll do really well, I'm sure."

"Thank you, President. As Kongzi would say, 'If you need a helping hand, take a look at the end of your arm'. Your association is the hand, Mr Lasalandra, and it is what the arm needs – and I am only its humble appendage."

"What a beautiful quotation, Mr Guo. I think we understand each other perfectly and we'll do a great job together."

"Of course we will. Now, if you would please forgive me, I need to take care of some business. But we'll be thoroughly prepared for the day after tomorrow."

"Wonderful. See you Thursday then."

"See you on Thursday, President, and thank you again."

"Thank you."

The black Jaguar was advancing smoothly, like a ship in a sea of sand. Snug in the back seat, Guo switched his phone off and sighed. The warmth from the air conditioning made the atmosphere most pleasant.

He was thinking about the stupid Italian *laowai*. Dirty foreign scum who hadn't yet grasped how little chance they had of survival. Sooner or later the great 14K Triad would subjugate them. And not only that. They were gullible and fell for everything he told them. He was no more than a speck in the great design of Sky, Earth and Man. He was ready to sacrifice his own and his nephew's lives to the Triad if necessary. In the name of a greater good, transcending the lives of individuals lost in the mists of time.

That's why how the day was going to end didn't matter too much. What really mattered was that he did his best to honour his number, 415, and his role as the White Paper Fan.

Pagnan was the final obstacle to their insidious takeover of the area. They'd stolen along the streets, a silent predator, relentless and lethal, devouring everything in its path one small bite at a time: bar after bar, shop after shop, restaurant after restaurant, until entire cities fell, one after the other.

He was getting close to the farmhouse. He had surprise on his side, a surprise that would cause quite a bit of strife for Pagnan and his men. He stretched his legs enjoying the warmth of the car while the Jaguar drove the last few yards to the meeting point.

Mila watched the car approaching.

She knew that hitting the target was possible,

but it wasn't going to be a walk in the park. It was six hundred yards away and she wasn't actually a professional sniper, although she had the skills to make the shot.

The challenge was that she'd have to fire one bullet after another without missing. The Chinese would take cover the second they heard the first shot coming in from behind them. Their cars were most likely bulletproof, so she needed to hit them fast and cause maximum damage before they could dive back inside.

Mule kept fidgeting with his Desert Eagle. He was staring at Mila, his eyes half closed, completely numb with the cold.

Mila waited.

She saw the two dark Jaguars parking in the farmyard. Pagnan was waiting outside, trying to look hard. Behind him Polenta and Tripe. To the side, a little to the right, Mila spotted Zhang, tied to the fence like a dog.

She concentrated and adjusted her zoom lens.

She saw the driver of the first car and the man who was riding shotgun get out. Four men from the second car. None of them was Guo.

Shit! Guo had to be the first she shot.

What if he'd decided to stay home?

"I can't see Guo," she said.

"You think he shat his pants and decided to stay

safely tucked up in his lair?" grunted Mule, who couldn't wait to put an end to this interminable waiting around.

"I don't think so. Let's see if he comes out. I have the feeling he'll be trying to screw us over."

"I don't trust that old asshole."

"And for once, we agree."

# 15

*BOOM!* The first shot.

The bullet took nearly half a second to cover the distance to its target. Its flight ended in Guo's back.

The Chinaman bent forward, his sunglasses flying in a gentle curve that ended in the mud of the farmyard.

His henchmen didn't have time to draw their weapons before a second shot split the sky and a bullet went through Guo's leg. The old man fell on his knees as a big, dark hole spurted blood all around him.

"Mila!" he screamed.

Uzis and automatics appeared in the hands of

his men. The former started pounding the air in short, deadly bursts. The latter started hurling bullets towards the windows of the farmhouse.

As soon as he'd heard the first shot, Pagnan had run towards the house.

Tripe and Polenta were slower and didn't take advantage of the element of surprise. They failed to move right away. Luckily, the Newbie and Pretty Boy joined in the action from behind the windows with their pump-action Maverick Mossberg .12s.

A bullet hit one of the Chinese in the throat. Instinctively he lifted his hand to his neck in an attempt to stop the bleeding. Screaming like a stuck pig, he crumpled to the ground and started thrashing about, trying to hold off the hand of death.

"Gaah!" he moaned before drawing his last breath.

Dry, sharp whistles cut through the air. Volleys of bullets whipped the ground.

Zhang covered his eyes and curled up, trying to make himself as small as he could. He leaned on the fence, desperately looking for some protection from the rain of bullets.

A third shot from somewhere opposite the farmhouse.

A couple of the Chinese turned in that

direction, swearing and exchanging quick nods.

"Die, you fucking yellow scumbags!"

Tripe's voice cut the air like a siren. His .50 Desert Eagle barked. A couple of bullets ended up in the leg of a Chinaman ahead of him. The gun kept clicking.

Next to him Polenta got nailed by a volley of .9mm bullets that literally lifted him from the ground and knocked him backwards. His body, hit repeatedly, spasmed as if someone had installed cables under his skin and turned on an electric current.

The courtyard looked like the OK Corral in Tombstone, where Wyatt Earp and Doc Holliday shot the Clanton brothers dead. But this wasn't the Wild West. It was the countryside just beyond Badia Polesine.

With a last-gasp leap, Pagnan jumped behind the door. Splinters of wood exploded all around him from the Uzis.

"Boss!" shouted the Newbie from inside the house while a hailstorm of broken glass tore at his clothes and unprotected skin. His voice reached a ridiculous pitch, even higher than the whistle of the bullets. He moved towards the entrance of the house to assist Pagnan's retreat and found himself in front of the doorway for a second. Unfortunately for him, the door was open.

He stood there like a hero.

Or a dumbass.

And was hit by an avalanche of bullets that butchered his chest. Red holes gaped on his white shirt. His feet started moving in a kind of a frantic breakdance.

Then he collapsed. First onto his knees, then his belly.

"No!" Pagnan shouted.


From on top of the old furnace Mila kept the bullets mercilessly raining down. Her shots were accurate. Steady. Undodgeable. Harvesting the lives of Guo's men like ears of wheat. Deadly trails cutting through the air and lodging between the shoulder blades of their victims. Fresh blood soaked the earth.

An apocalypse of violence. Screams, agony, broken lives. One after another. One next to another.

Caught in the middle, the Triads couldn't turn the situation around. Targeted by the crossfire of Pretty Boy's Mossberg and Mila's Beretta, they had no chance of finding shelter.

Two of them had tried to get back to the car but Mila hit them from above. Stars of blood and brain matter burst out of their heads.

Miraculously, Tripe was still standing. He was

bleeding from an arm that had been grazed by a bullet.

Guo was crawling towards Zhang, who was still curled up near the fence. Each movement Guo made was a struggle. Each yard a jolt of pain shot through his entire body, making him shudder. A dying rat with no way out.

Zhang lifted his head and saw him a few yards away. A handless puppet, Zhang was crying big-time, heavy tears running down his pale near-blue cheeks. His jaw had been clenched for over fifteen hours, and now seemed to give his face an expression that suggested the desperation of a life slipping away.

That woman is a devil, he thought.

She had humiliated them and torn them to pieces. Again. And now there was nothing to be done except watch his uncle crawl towards him like a worm, bloody and exhausted.

He held out his arm, or what was left of it, tried to stretch as much as the rope around his neck allowed. The muscles in his neck were tighter than ever.

"Forgive me, uncle," he managed to whisper.

"Za... ng," Guo whispered back. A second later the White Paper Fan of the 14K Triad, leader of the Talking Daggers, lowered his eyes. For the last time.

• • •

Pagnan picked up the Newbie's Mossberg and drilled the back of the last Chinaman standing. The man fell forward, his arms spread out, a Christ crashing onto the hard, cold ground in a stew of red blood.

"Yahoo!" shouted Pagnan, happiness in his eyes. The eyes of a child whose grandfather had just given him the bar of chocolate he demanded.

Pretty Boy stared at him in disbelief. On the ground next to them was the dead body of the Newbie. Riddled by a dozen gunshots.

Tripe was coughing.

"Are you all right?" Pagnan asked him.

"Yes boss! Fuck! There's nothing we can do for Polenta."

"Shit, I know! The Newbie's gone too…"

"He died saving your ass," remarked Pretty Boy.

"Hey, I know, don't think I don't! Yes, he saved my ass. And I won't forget. Anyway, better the Newbie than me. What, you want me to write a song for him?"

"Pfff!" replied Pretty Boy, and wiped the sweat from his forehead with his right forearm. The tension that had been building up had exploded in a huge adrenaline rush.

Tripe looked around. "Fucking hell! It's a blood-bath out here!"

It felt like he had gotten back in touch with

reality after a mental short circuit a few minutes long. After the blackout, his thoughts had immediately turned to the wound on his arm.

He'd examined it and judged it not too serious. He'd taken off his jacket and his shirt and torn the latter to pieces, ripped it into strips and tied them together to make a long bandage which he'd then wrapped around the wound.

Pagnan saw Zhang bent over his uncle's lifeless body. He picked up his mobile and called Mule, who answered after three rings.

"You see that, boss? The babe here's slaughtered them!"

"Yes, she has. Where were you?"

"What do you mean, boss? I was here with her, on the roof of the furnace. Without a zoom lens and with all the carnage down there, I'm not entirely sure what the fuck exactly happened."

"Those bastards killed Polenta and the Newbie."

"Shit. Sons of bitches."

"I know. Certainly could have gone better. Or worse. Listen," said Pagnan, "get your ass into gear. There's a stack of corpses to tidy up."

"Cool, on our way."

Mule ended the conversation and turned to Mila. She was busy taking the zoom lens off the rifle with precise, robotic movements. Unfaltering, emotionless. She could have been forged in iron.

"How do you do it?" Mule asked.

"How do I do what?" replied Mila.

"I mean… you just caused a massacre with that fucking alien-killer of a space gun and… well…"

"What do you think I *should* be doing?"

"I don't know… maybe sighing a little or something. But no reaction? *Nada*? I'd love to know how the fuck you do it."

"Huh. Those were criminals, not nurses."

"OK, OK, forget about it…"

"A little late to get all sentimental, Mule, don't you think? You should have thought about it earlier. Anyway, they're the ones who started this war."

"True that. Hey, I wasn't criticising you. Actually I have to admit you did an awesome job. Don't be pissed off."

"You know your whinging's pretty insufferable?"

"Oi, kid, you're the one who's insufferable!" replied Mule wiping his forehead, soaked in a cold sweat.

Once she'd finished taking the rifle apart, Mila put everything back in the two bags. They shouldered them and climbed down the crumbling staircase. Around them, what had once been the rooms in which bricks were heated now looked like ancient stone relics. Simulacrums destroyed by time, silent witnesses to future events.

Mule stood behind Mila and unholstered his Desert Eagle while she removed the tarpaulin hiding the Ford Focus and opened the boot.

Something darted through the air. Initially Mule couldn't work out what that long stick that was about to hit him might be. By the time he got it, it was too late.

He felt a blinding pain in the pit of his stomach and bent forwards, looking up at the girl, his eyes screaming in pain. He felt his strength leave him, his legs start to bend.

One more whistle through the air.

Diagonal upwards blow, right to left.

*Crack.*

Mila had taken a hockey stick from the boot, where it had lain hidden under a blanket. Sixty-five inches of seriously hard wood. A white inscription in the cobalt blue of the stick: Bauer.

The stick was now stained with Mule's blood.

"God!" he shouted. Lying on his back, he moved his arms and legs like a flipped-over tortoise. Mila was pressing on his stomach with her leather boot, staring at him with her green eyes, as if trying to hypnotise him. "Fuck you."

"Never learn, will you? You're too old for me, Mule. Thought I'd already told you."

The man coughed. "Dirty bitch!"

"You're a bitch in heat, a cocksucking slut who likes to get fucked," added Mila with a strange tone to her voice.

"What?"

"You're a bitch in heat, a cocksucking slut who likes to get fucked. You remember those words, you bastard?"

Mule still didn't understand. He kept blinking.

"Those are the words you grunted in my ear while you raped me. After you murdered my father."

"What the fuck are you talking about?"

"What the fuck am I talking about? Tell me, you remember that policeman you and three other of your boss' fucking underlings killed twelve years ago while robbing a restaurant in Padua? You went to jail for that job, wouldn't think you'd forget about it."

Mule's eyes lit up. "Ah, the little girl…"

"Yes, *the little girl*."

"That… that was you?"

As he spoke the words he realised with absolute certainty that he was going to die.

Mila didn't reply. Her eyes narrowed to cracks. She raised her clenched fists to her hips in an instinctive action, born out of the rage that the memory still caused in her. But she didn't speak.

She kept staring at her father's murderer.

"You remember it so clearly. Sounds like maybe you enjoyed what I did to you," said Mule chuckling and trying to get back on his feet. He thought he was making some headway; the girl seemed to be in a trance.

Enraged, Mila grabbed him around the hips, shoved him against the Focus and started going to work on him. Her punches hammered Mule's chest with a steady rhythm that knocked the wind out of his lungs. She kept hitting him methodically, making sure that each and every one of his ribs had the pleasure of becoming acquainted with her knuckles.

Then she paused to allow him to catch his breath. She crouched in front of him and stared right in his eyes.

"Now I want to know one thing."

"Ask away, bitch."

"Before you croak, tell me who ordered you to kill my father."

"You already know."

"I want to hear you say it."

"Why? What for?"

"If you don't tell me, I'll start again."

Mule breathed in slowly and summoned up the last of his strength.

"Rossano Pagnan."

"What a surprise."

"I'd never seen him as upset as he was back then."

"I can imagine."

"He kept saying he had a problem with a cop. A problem as big as his fucking fat belly." Mule managed a smile. Then he coughed and wiped his lips with an arm, trying to remove the red drool that was slurring up his words.

"What did he tell you? I mean, what did he say when he ordered you to murder my father?"

"It was the four of us with him. Myself and the three who're still in jail."

"Forget about them. Go on."

"Well, he told us that a police detective was on his back. His name was…"

"Giorgio Zago."

"Exactly. He said that Zago was a tough nut, one he couldn't make a deal with. And that Zago was getting too close to his business. We were running the risk of having to shut up shop…"

"Then what?"

Mule spat. Talking was becoming a torture. But Mila was looming over him.

"He told us he'd tried to give him one of his 'care packages', one of those offers you can't refuse, full of money."

"But it came to nothing, right?"

"Right."

"So he sent you to that restaurant, Da Renzo. To kick the owner's ass and kill my father."

"Yes."

"Anything to add?" said Mila. "Because I have to tell you, you'll be gone very soon."

"Fuck you."

"So be it."

Mila lifted her gaze to the sky. She took one of the two .45s from the boot of the Focus and screwed the silencer on it.

She looked at Mule one last time.

"Have a nice trip, Lover Boy."

*Clunk*!

A lead slug went into his forehead.

File closed.

# 16

It was getting cold.

The grey land was preparing to get frosted over. A barren plain except for a few clumps of grass poking through the ground in the area surrounding the furnace, the soil rock-hard beneath the darkening sky.

Mila had worn her leather jacket and her yellow specs. Five foot seven of muscle primed to join the action. The Colt .45s jiggled on her hips. Her red dreadlocks looked increasingly like fiery snakes on the head of a third-millennium Medusa.

A Queen of Death ready for her final mission.

Four hundred yards.

The shadowy plain was now a combat zone. In front of her, Pagnan's farmhouse.

Mila savoured the moment she'd been waiting for.

The final showdown. After more than ten years.

Two hundred yards.

She could now see the Chinamen's cars clearly. Big, empty Jaguars, the doors wide open.

One hundred yards.

She was drawing closer with all the boldness of a predator that had just smelled fresh meat.

Fifty yards.

Now she could make out more details of the massacre. Pools of blood, bodies torn apart. Proper carnage.

Twenty yards.

In front of her, a man. *That man*.

Rossano Pagnan looked at her with his dark, piggy eyes. Next to him, Tripe and Pretty Boy.

Mila and Pagnan stared at each other. His hair was a tangled mess, black streaked with grey; his almost-white goatee reminded her of an old wolf about to attack.

"You're alone, are you?" said Pagnan. "You think I wasn't expecting it? Think you surprised me? Expect me to be speechless because you took out Mule, that useless halfwit? Is that what you think?" He pointed the Mossberg calibre .12 at her.

"What I think doesn't matter much. And what you think matters fuck all. As usual, while you're wittering away you're missing the important stuff. Typical of a dipshit like you. You never realised who I was. And that condemned you right from the off. You were already dead before you got here and you didn't know it. You're an asshole, Rossano Pagnan."

"My God, I'm quaking in my boots. Right, guys? You lads shitting your pants too?" replied Pagnan, his voice a couple of notches too high. It reached Mila's ears cracking with tension, even though he was trying hard to keep it steady.

"Sure, boss. My legs are shaking," said Pretty Boy, his long hair in a tangle with dust and sweat, his blue apron stained with blood.

"I'm scared too!" added Tripe.

"Fuck off, old man," said Mila.

The Colt .45s sprung out of their holsters.

Four blasts ripped the air. Two from each gun. Supersonic speed.

A pair of red stains appeared on Pretty Boy's chest; he spun around like a bowling pin and crumpled over, his flesh torn apart. A spasm, then nothing more. Smoke curled out of his torso where the bullets had entered.

Tripe had a hole near his heart and he just couldn't believe it. He was trying to staunch the wound with his hand but the blood was gushing out.

"Shit… aargh!" he grunted, already on his knees.

An instant later he crashed face-first into the mud.

The fourth bullet had shattered Pagnan's right kneecap. He'd gone down and was gasping like a fish that's jumped out of its bowl.

"Mila… you fucking bitch…" He tried to raise his Mossberg but she kicked it away.

"Why the fuck are you doing this to me?" he shouted.

"You want to know *now*? Too late! Did you think you had me in your pocket? You didn't have a chance in Hell, you poor old idiot."

"I'm not old…"

"You destroyed my life, you old fuck."

Pagnan couldn't avoid looking at Mila's hair. It was flashing red against the evening sky.

"You killed my father, got your men to rape me, ripped out everything good I had inside me and left me with nothing but hate."

Mila started to cry. She felt the weight of the world slowly leave her as the tears fell. A dark pain she'd kept chained up for too long started to leak through the cracks in her armour. And she was already beginning to feel the disappointment of realising that the moment she'd been waiting all this time for wouldn't give her the relief she'd hoped for.

Rossano Pagnan, weak and desperate, looked at her through his own tears, and muttered, "It's not true... Why are you saying this? Who was your father? Who are you?"

"Twelve years ago your men robbed a restaurant in Padua. It ended in slaughter. I was there too, dining with my father. They riddled him with bullets, showed no mercy. He was a policeman, and you had him killed because you were afraid he'd nail you."

"Christ!" said Pagnan. "That fucking restaurant robbery!"

He remembered, sure. And now, with his life in the balance, he also recalled the big, green eyes of that little girl staring at him, terrified, during the trial. That's where he'd seen her before.

"I had nothing to do with it," he tried to say. "I wasn't even there..." He coughed. "Believe me, Mila. Even the judge confirmed that, don't you remember?"

Then he looked at her, his eyes wide, like a small child who sees, in the darkness of his bedroom, a sliver of light through the open door.

"Bastard!" shouted Mila in his face. She got closer and kicked him in the chest.

"Mi... Mila... listen, I have money... please don't kill me. I had nothing to do with that incident. There must be some mistake." Pagnan coughed, nearly choked.

"You're trying to make a deal? Seriously? Don't you feel invincible any longer without your two-bit mercenaries? You honestly think you can buy me off? Fuck you, Pagnan."

"I'm sorry, I didn't know."

Mila shook her head. Her rage was turning to nausea. She'd imagined this very scene thousands of times over the years, and she never thought she'd feel like this.

Disgust, that's what it was. A feeling that manifested itself through a slow, constantly growing burning pain in her chest.

Rossano Pagnan was simply a coward. A weak, ingratiating little man unable to play his role of villain, of criminal, of killer. A greedy little man who had flicked a switch and taken her father's life through somebody else's hands.

The tragedy of her life now sounded like a joke to Mila's ears, a mean prank played by fate. This was a sad, pathetic conclusion to a story that in her opinion deserved to be played out by very different characters.

There was nothing epic in Pagnan's wickedness.

And she would have to make him suffer for that inadequacy too.

"God, this is vile," she barked through clenched teeth. "At least try to keep a little dignity. You make me want to heave."

Pagnan didn't reply, hiding behind a fear-induced silence.

"You don't think it's already over, do you?" she prodded him. "Stand up, little man. Show me you still have some guts."

But he didn't move. Other than to tremble.

Mila couldn't believe what she was seeing.

"Man up. Get to your feet, you fucker!"

She took him by the shoulders and turned him around, forcing him onto his back. At that second, she felt that she was crossing a line to a place from where there was no return.

It felt like a blade was scraping across her heart. A metallic pain, along with the awareness that her soul was now irretrievably rotten. What she had done until now was nothing compared to what she was about to do.

She bent over Pagnan. She grabbed the lapels of his shirt collar and pulled, ripping it off him, from top to bottom, the buttons popping off. Then she took him by the neck and sat him up.

Tugged his mud-stained black jacket down, baring his shoulders, and then pinched his nipples between finger and thumb and twisted hard. She yanked upwards, forcing him to his feet.

Pagnan felt like a bucket of boiling oil had been thrown over his chest. His body would go wherever she guided it. No choice.

A rag doll in Mila's hands.

But maybe he could still talk his way out, if it wasn't already too late. With a little luck he might be able to reach one of the guns he'd spotted earlier, discarded on the ground not too far away. He needed to draw this out.

Mila's face drew closer to his.

"Open your eyes," she said.

Pagnan blinked faintly.

"Open your eyes!" she repeated.

This time he obeyed, taking his time about it, though – to Mila it felt like a slice of eternity. His eyes, wide open, got lost in hers, an emerald sea shining with liquid yellow light.

They were not a woman's eyes any longer.

They were the eyes of a Fury.

"Listen, Mila. I didn't want your father to die. It was my men, they lost their heads! Yes, they were working for me, but I'd given them detailed instructions: rob the restaurant. Nothing else! I don't know what came over them…"

"You expect me to believe that?"

"Mila, you have to believe me…"

"I don't have to do anything."

"Please, think about what you're doing. You're not a cold-blooded killer."

"What the fuck do you know about me, you old wanker? Do you have the slightest inkling of what you turned me into?"

"No, I don't. But I'm realising that you wanted to arrange a bloodbath between us and them."

"You got it, pal! Took you long enough."

"So? Haven't you seen enough blood? Don't you think it's time to stop?"

"Not when I'm about to tuck into the main course. *You're* the main course, old man. It's useless to try to buy yourself time."

"I'm just trying to explain how things are."

"Too bad you already took everything from me that I hold dear, and you can't rewind the clock. So cut the crap."

"Please, Mila!"

"I hope you enjoy Hell."

Pagnan couldn't think, much less talk. Terror had obliterated his thoughts and silenced his tongue.

He whimpered, a dull sound, interrupted by tears.

"Shit! I have to do everything myself," said Mila. She lifted him onto his feet and spat in his face. Then she punched him.

Pagnan crumbled to the ground.

An enormous, fat octopus. A shadow of a man.

Punching Pagnan gave Mila renewed energy. She felt it flowing back through her arm. Like a backdraft.

She hit him again. And again. And again.

She grabbed him by the hair and dragged him to one of the cars.

Pagnan yelled, then Mila lifted him back onto his feet.

"It's your time. Let's end this."

"No, please!"

"Shut up."

"No, I beg you… you can't…"

She took one of the Colts and pushed it against his belly.

*Bang!*

*Bang!*

*Bang!*

Dark blood squirted out.

A rotten watermelon exploding, ruptured by bullets.

Rossano Pagnan looked at her one last time. His eyes wide open, his mouth agape, his hands clawing the air to try to catch a last breath, a little more life.

"Bye bye, old man," said Mila.

# 17

Zhang couldn't believe his eyes when he saw Guo stand up, just a few yards away.

He looked at him, petrified.

Guo took his tie off and tightened it around his left thigh, where the bullet had dug a small, bloody tunnel. Then he took off his jacket, his shirt and the Kevlar body armour that had stopped the first bullet, the one that had hit him in the back. He stood there, bare-chested, in the freezing night.

A blue bruise ten inches wide discoloured his back at the spot where the bullet had hit the body armour.

His pale chest was marked by long thin lines

scarring his skin and telling many stories about his life.

Mila looked at him, nodding.

"Welcome back to the living," she told him.

Guo turned to face her. "As we agreed, right?"

"Sorry I hit you in the leg, but I couldn't risk Pagnan's men smelling a rat."

"No problem, I understand. So what do we do now, you and I?"

"What do you mean?"

"I mean, you let me live and I let you live? Or do you have something else in mind?"

"Listen here, Guo: I wanted to kill your men *anyway*. My mission is to clean up this land."

"Oh, that's how it goes, is it? You're a knight in shining armour now?"

"If that's how you want to put it. But the men you sent to my home to kill me deserved what they got. Your nephew included. And those I killed today weren't innocent little lambs either."

"Looks like everything is very clear in your mind."

"Yep. We both know perfectly well who you are and what you do. The Talking Daggers are taking over Veneto. The way I look at it, you're nothing more or less than any other criminal organisation: Sicilian mafia, Chinese mafia,

Neapolitan camorra or Calabrian 'ndrangheta – it's all the same to me. Let's just say that I started a personal vendetta and that the dead are simply casualties of war."

"I see," said Guo. "A wise man acts and then talks, and his talk follows his actions."

"Couldn't have said it better."

"Still, you shot my leg."

"Right. But I'm ready to even the odds."

As she spoke, Mila pointed one of the .45s against her left thigh.

A look.

*Bang!*

A shot.

The bullet pierced her thigh, about six inches above the knee.

"Now we're even. You're an honourable man. For a criminal. And I don't need an advantage to defeat you."

Guo didn't say anything, but his eyes revealed his surprise.

He looked around.

A couple of yards away he saw a piece of wood that looked long and thick enough.

He got closer to it. With a sudden but premeditated move, he dug his toes underneath it and flicked it up towards his chest, then grabbed it with both hands.

Mila didn't waste any time getting into position.

She took a half step to her left so that her feet were the same width apart as her shoulders. She brought her hands to her hips, fists clenched, palms up, then straightened her shoulders, keeping her forearms parallel.

"Shaolin kung fu," said Guo. "*Wu Bu Quan*, the form of the five steps. *Qi Shi*, the first movement. Well executed, too."

Mila stared at him, waiting for his next move. Her face was like a sphinx. Etched in stone.

She didn't show any emotion.

Guo narrowed his eyes and started running, the stick held low, his right hand above the left. When he got close to Mila he drove the stick into the ground in a smooth and surprisingly nimble movement. He spun quickly and somersaulted, using all his momentum to bring the stick smashing down.

Mila didn't fall for it. She didn't turn, only a minimal movement to dodge the blow. Then she shifted her weight onto her left leg, adopting the archer position, and threw a punch, keeping her arm level with her shoulder.

Guo's nose broke in a tremendous cracking of destroyed cartilage.

Off-balance because of the missed strike and

thumped square in the face by Mila's punch, he tried to get back into position with a butterfly jump.

But while he was trying to regain his balance, the woman had already started another attack. With a double leap forward, ignoring the pain that bit into her leg, she maintained her distance from her opponent and then completed the move with a third jump during which she spun around to finish it off, as she went down, with a perfect blow to Guo's neck: the deadliest *xuan feng jiao* ever executed in Veneto.

*Crack!*

The collarbone of the Chinaman shattered under the devastating kick. A second later he was nothing but a rag doll lying on the ground in an unnatural position.

Only then did Mila take some time to bandage her wound. Then she threw a last look towards Zhang: she'd already decided she would leave him there, tied to the fence, to bleed to death.

She had filmed the whole fight with the video camera in her specs. Now she only needed some luck and hoped that the footage she'd collected would be enough to interest Joch Unterberger, BHEG High Commander and close friend of her grandfather's.

# 18

Mila got back to her car.

Her leg was really hurting now.

It had been bloody stupid to shoot herself in the thigh.

But she wanted to prove to the world that she was as tough as they came.

Her father and grandfather would have been proud of her, and that was good enough for her.

Now she felt at peace. Dog-tired and bleeding from the thigh wound, but her mind was carefree. She'd faced her foe in a fair fight and she'd won. Without cheating. Following the rules.

There was one last thing she had to do. But until then, she just had to rest for a week and wait.

She put everything she needed in the boot and headed north.

Mr Carraro, the lawyer, would receive her journal in a few days. He'd deliver it to Chiara Berton, the Public Prosecutor, within five days after that. Even if they started looking for her right away, they'd never find her. Not in such a short time. Not in such a wild place.

She drove up the Bassa from Badia Polesine and headed towards Trento through Solesino, Cittadella and Bassano del Grappa. Then the Valsugana opened before her like a Dolomian mountain wall in the crust of the Earth. Hard, harsh folds in the stony bed of the Brenta river.

When she got to the Scale di Primolano, on top of which was the war memorial, Mila turned left and drove up the snaking concrete road that would bring her, sixteen hairpin bends later, to Enego.

The automatic gearbox allowed her to keep her leg still, but she had no doubts that it was getting worse. She needed to get to her destination as soon as possible. She started the CD player.

Tom Waits started to sing about red roses and golden bullets, and it felt for a moment as if the tension was dissipating. Dark sky, deep green pine trees, the naked branches of the larches, snow falling from above like candyfloss, that strong, sweet smell. The moss-paved undergrowth poked out at her along the road to Mount Lisser. She yawned. Everything spelled sleep. But both the pain and her survival instinct helped keep her awake.

About twenty minutes later she saw the familiar outline of her cabin. She parked behind it. Took one of the tennis bags from the boot.

It was 8 in the evening.

She went inside and walked to the bathroom. Took what she needed to medicate herself out of the medicine cabinet. Removed her clothes and got in the tub, letting the water wash over her, even though it was bloody cold.

She tried to move her leg to evaluate the damage. Clots of blood, shredded skin and pieces of flesh came off, reddening the water. The bullet hole was the size of a hazelnut. She grabbed the bottle of grappa she'd taken with her and knocked back a couple of mouthfuls.

A few minutes later, she got out of the tub and splashed her leg liberally with alcohol. Then she used tweezers to remove the tiny pieces of skin and burned flesh still attached to the edges of the wound. She staunched it with a clean towel and put gauze dressings on the entry and exit wounds. She filled a plastic syringe with an antibiotic. Then she drank a couple more mouthfuls of grappa. She inserted the needle in her thigh muscle and pressed gently. She got ready for bed with a heavy dose of painkillers.

The following morning she woke up pretty late. She got out of bed and clumped on a pair of crutches over to the tennis bag. She fished out her Macbook and specs, plugged the specs into her computer and downloaded all the clips, adding the earlier closed-circuit camera recordings.

She emailed the lot of them. It took a while.

Now she just had to wait.

# 19

*From Mila Zago's journal:*

So, this is the end.

I'm a little sorry about that, actually. It's the same feeling I get when I reach the last page of an Emilio Salgari swashbuckler. Do you know him? Sandokan, the Black Corsair…? I frequently re-read those novels. My father gave them to me when I was a kid. Salgari is really good. He never travelled but was able to build a highly believable world. His novels are full of pirates boarding enemy ships, swords, guns, killings. I wasn't born when the

television series about the Tiger of
Mompracem – the one with Kabir Bedi in
it – was shown. I watched it a few years
later, when RAI re-ran it on prime time.

Sorry, I'm rambling, apologies.

Let's try to reconstruct recent events.

I'm sure you have already found out that
the slaughter in Limenella Nord a couple of
days ago is linked to the Badia Polesine
massacre. If by any chance you were not
aware of that yet, let me confirm it: yes,
the two events are closely linked. It all
stemmed from bad blood between the
Chinese and Rossano Pagnan's gang.
Competition in a free market, you know
how it is. Of course I hardly need say that I
took full advantage of the situation. I pitted
one group against the other and I made
sure they annihilated each other. Neat, eh?
Of course they were a big help.

I'll keep the details brief.

Ottorino Longhin, one of Pagnan's men,
betrayed his side and sold out to Guo
Xiaoping, the 14K White Paper Fan and
leader of the Talking Daggers. I trust those
names mean something to you, Dr Berton?
Anyway, in Limenella Nord, it was
Longhin who killed Marco and Mirco

Galesso, the twin accountants who took care of laundering Pagnan's money and who, incidentally, had two million in cash stowed in the boot of their Mercedes the day they were shot.

In Limenella, Longhin lost it. And caused a needless massacre.

That's when I stepped in.

I protected the weak and oppressed and delivered Longhin to the police. Pretty efficient of me, don't you think? Of course, as soon as Pagnan found out what had happened he went completely berserk. He sent his men to pick up the traitor at the Padua hospital. The kidnapping was successful. They killed a few people and brought Longhin to Pagnan, who tortured him within an inch of his life without managing to get a single word out of him.

After capturing the nephew of the bad old Chinaman, I returned to the scene. Doesn't matter how I caught him. I don't want to bore you with the details.

I proposed an agreement between the two bosses. Like you would in court.

Anyway, a deal was on the cards. Guo was ready to meet Pagnan to have his nephew back, as he loved him like a son. He promised to withdraw quietly from the Veneto underworld, keeping a small piece of the drugs market but letting go of everything else. He would have accepted some self-imposed limitations, not unlike the Indians in their reservations after their dealings with the white man.

Of course Pagnan didn't trust him.

The funny thing in all this mess is that I was behind it all. I knew where Pagnan's two million euros were and I was holding Zhang Wen, the Chinaman's nephew. So Pagnan needed to listen to me, to trust me, if he wanted to see his money again. And Guo too, he had to do the same if he wanted to see his nephew alive.

We're nearly there.

The venue for the meeting: Pagnan's farmhouse near Badia Polesine.

First Pagnan gets there with his men. And me, of course.

Then the Chinese arrive.

The shit hits the fan. Predictable, right? There's a major shootout, and at the end the only two people left standing are Guo and me. Zhang Wen is also still alive, but he's on his knees, tied to a fence.

How did it end? Well, you'll see when you get there.

Guo, well, I left him in a bad way.

Zhang should still be tied up. You'll notice that his hands are missing, and I imagine that the stumps might have turned gangrenous despite being cauterised. Most likely he'll have died of blood loss, though.

So, that's a short summary of events.

In the envelope that Mr Carraro, the lawyer, will hand to you, you'll also find, along with my journal, a key for a locker which you'll find in Marco Polo airport, terminal 2. It's number 136. There you'll find a Nike tennis bag, and inside the bag is the money. Well, some of it. I kept a bit. Expenses, you know.

I think that's all. Pretty much. You can find out the rest yourself. Let's face it, you get paid a silly amount, don't you? Time you earned it. I read somewhere that someone had taken to calling you magistrates an "uber-clique". I don't know if it's true, but I don't think it was entirely made up by an over-imaginative journalist.

Ah, one last thing: don't bother trying to find me. First of all, you won't. Second, you have all the details you need to put the entire case to bed. Third: believe it or not, you and I are on the same side.

OK, so I'm a little meaner than you. Anyway, don't worry, you'll see: if I need to get in touch with you I'll manage.

Ah, and – don't forget – go to Hodegart and watch the Asiago Lions. Promise me that. And when you get there buy a red and yellow scarf and drink a warm VOV and brandy cocktail. You're from Vicenza, aren't you? You can't miss such a fine spectacle. You never know, we might even bump into one another.

Anyway, now I have to say goodbye. Thanks for everything. And don't be too mad at me.

Lots of love,


Mila

# 20

Like a stone sentry on a buttress, Schloss Eisturm dominated the valley. A medieval castle, its battlements outlined against the sky. Under the stronghold, a narrow road left the main pass through the valley and climbed to the summit of a peaked hill.

Plinths of ice embellished the view. A white quilt of snow covered the valley, blanketing all sound and creating a fairytale atmosphere. The branches of the spruce trees were so heavy with snow that they seemed close to breaking point. A surreal silence hovered over the scene.

The streams were veins, hardened by the cold. They crisscrossed the land's white skin and threaded the slopes in dark bands of motionless water.

Oberammergau, the Alpine Road, the German Alps.

The chimneys of the castle blew gentle smoke that curled in white swirls filling the air with candyfloss clouds. The huge glass windows of the barbican contrasted with the dark stone of the stronghold. They reflected the light of the big chandeliers and shone like evil eyes spying on any travellers who might walk through the narrow, desolate valley.

Inside one of the rooms in the barbican, a man.

Joch Unterberger couldn't shift his gaze from the screen.

He couldn't believe his eyes.

The girl had tons of talent. Technically perfect, savage, bloodthirsty: she had the potential to become the best bounty hunter in the Guild. The perfect professional to cover the area comprising the north-east of Italy, Tirol and Austria. Then, maybe after she'd gained some experience tackling those maniacs from the Schwarzer Adler – a gang of madmen whose headquarters the Guild had been unable to locate; they were systematically disseminating their unique brand of Nazi-Fascism – she might slowly mature into one of their global agents, one of those who could tackle the most dangerous of missions anywhere in Europe.

The video clips she'd just sent him – virtually a snuff movie – were really, really enthralling. Breathtaking.

The girl had style. Damn right she did. She was fast, those red dreadlocks whipping the air. She didn't so much kill her victims as grind them to a pulp. The Guild needed agents like her. Joch was watching a clip where she confronted three Chinese in a confined space. She moved like a wild cat, slicing through arms and legs with her katana in a deadly dance that gave him the shivers. What elegance! What fluidity!

Unterberger was already eating his third slice of Black Forest gateau: chocolate and cherries. And he couldn't stop. He was forgetting all about his body, the slim, toned physique he'd counted on for years and years while he busted his balls to gather experience, money and contacts to make his dream come true: a private guild at the service of – and sponsored by – the most important entrepreneurs in Europe aimed at totally wiping organised crime from the face of the map.

Lacking any effective organisation, both at a national and international level, many voices speculated that maybe it was time to go back to the old ways. The European Union was, after all, proof positive of how member countries were failing to cooperate on the justice front. Too many problems associated with differences in judicial systems, too many power plays, too much red tape.

However, security was and remained vital. So vital that politicians weren't going to get in the way. Through a series of hidden funds, several professional associations and groups of economic and financial players had helped create an EC-wide security organisation. Private. Nothing official, of course: that wouldn't be sufficiently politically correct.

From the diamond producers in Antwerp to the big multinational companies, everyone had agreed that Europe needed some kind of private security association. Thus, the BHEG was born. The BHEG – the Bounty Hunters European Guild – had been active for some time now. Following the American example.

It was impossible to find the Guild, but the Guild could find anyone it wanted to. A group of veterans and mercenaries from the Grenzschutz-gruppe 9, the Spetsnaz, the Alpini, the ROS, the Korps Commandotroepen and Her Majesty's Secret Service. Hand-picked personnel who received six months training in the snow-clad Urals and German Alpine Road.

Due to his impressive CV, Joch Unterberger had naturally become the leader of that secret army.

He was staring at his computer screen, eyes open wide like a chameleon on acid, admiring what his old Italian friend Gastone Zago had created.

The perfect warrior.

The perfect warrior was a woman called Mila Zago.

Frank van Eick silently entered Unterberger's office. It was small but comfortable, sparsely furnished: some oak bookshelves, a mahogany coffee-table, a couple of comfortable leather armchairs in front of a fireplace piled high with burning logs. In front of it, the desk on which Joch had placed a twenty-two-inch flatscreen monitor.

"On you go!" he shouted.

"I can't fail to notice a certain degree of enthusiasm, Joch. What's happened?" asked van Eick, relaxed and composed as ever.

"Ah, it's you, my old friend," replied Unterberger getting close to the screen, as if he was planning on eating it.

"What are you watching?"

"The most beautiful, lethal fighting machine

you've ever seen. Come closer. Take a look at her in action."

Van Eick followed his suggestion and approached the screen.

He saw a redhead in a latex suit leaping around wielding a curved Japanese sword. She landed behind someone who looked like an Asian assassin, flexed her knees and hit the Asian's leg with a roundhouse kick that brought him down. Impressive. Her speed of reaction and the precision of her moves were close to perfection.

And it wasn't over: as the killer's face was falling towards the tiles, she lowered the katana and sliced upwards, left to right.

The head of the Asian came clean off his torso and flew through the air in a bright red geyser, coming to rest next to another corpse lying on the floor.

"My God!" said van Eick. "Is this real?"

Unterberger looked at his colleague with satisfaction.

"Isn't she something?" he said with a broad smile.

"She's a psychopath! I mean, don't you think she's just a bit… over the top?"

"Well, yes, she's playing to the camera. But she's very good."

"Where's she from?"

"Italy."

"Hm. A race of useless scum. Nothing but thieves and beggars."

"And traitors."

"Right."

"Still, she could be Turkish or Greek, wouldn't change a thing. I was thinking of letting her loose in the area between the north-east of Italy and Austria. Ever since they killed Blue Eyes, we've had no presence there."

"You're hiring her?"

"I'll give her a test first. She's not a run-of-the-mill mercenary joining us from some special corps. She's pure talent. A wild horse. And self-taught, too. Well, not really…"

"What do you mean 'not really'?"

"She was brought up by an old friend of mine from World War II."

"I concede, the girl's impressive. If this is real. Sure it's not from a computer game?"

"It's all original, live footage."

"And who recorded it?"

"She did. You know how youngsters are. They film everything."

"She's definitely a psycho."

"I've made my decision. We'll give her a test. I already have a codename for her."

"Really? What?"

"Something poetic, yet threatening. Something fierce and deadly."

"Cut the crap and spit it out."

"Red Dread."

"Red Dread?"

"Yes, Red Dread."

"Well, to be fair, it fits."

"Doesn't it?"

"Now calm down."

"Right, I'll calm down, but you call her. And make sure you use an untraceable mobile."

"Joch, I'm not a schoolboy."

"Tell her to be at the Slaughtered Roe Inn at noon on Saturday"

"She looks like a monumental dose of trouble."

"So what? We're not looking for someone to bake us cupcakes. Just call her."

"OK."

Joch Unterberger smiled. After an awful day, the evening looked much more promising. That girl was a godsend. She would produce results in the badlands of the north-east of Italy, Tirol and Austria. Under siege from immigrants, ravaged by racial clashes, the denizens of that area were among the main contributors to the Guild. Ever since Blue Eyes had been branded with a swastika and killed, the area was getting less and less safe. They needed to get on top of the situation as soon as possible.

Mila Zago was the right person for the job.

The days of the Schwarzer Adler were numbered. Of that, he was certain.

He cut one more slice of the gateau and carried it from the tray to the small Bavarian porcelain plate. The chocolate was wonderful, and the cream – made from fresh, frothy milk from German cows – was delicious. Soft, smooth, irresistible.

Oral sex for the taste buds.

# 21

Chiara Berton stared at the stiff canvas cover of the notebook she was holding in her hands. She leaned against the back of her leather chair, stretched her shapely legs under her desk and sighed.

Towers of files and briefs covered the entire surface of her work desk, and the sprawl continued onto the floor. Folder after folder, one after another, on top of one another, in no order whatsoever.

Amidst that ocean of documentation, the lawyer – Carraro – had brought her the diary. He told her he wanted to make sure nobody else would see it. Then he added that he didn't know what was in it.

Along with the diary there was also a small key,
probably for a locker.

She yawned.

She was half-asleep. She sometimes asked
herself why she found her job so special. But she
knew the answer, and it had nothing to do with
anything that could be found in a procedural
manual.

Sure, she worked in criminal law, but
ultimately what she really liked was the chance
to deal with the worst side of people, men and
women, day after day. It was neither a sadistic nor
masochistic pleasure, simply that she believed
someone should be responsible for defining the
boundaries of abnormal behaviour. By applying
the law, of course.

There was also an undeniable narcissistic
element. The work gratified her and kept her in
check, because it gave her the chance to enjoy
visibility, respect, attention. She was a woman in
what was still very much a man's world, and
having power and being popular were some kind
of reward, especially given that she had built her
career brick by brick, with no easy shortcuts. She
was still good-looking, mind you, which probably
gave her an advantage with lawyers, judges and
maybe even the occasional defendant.

She went back to the small blue notebook. She

slid her hand under the rubberband that kept it closed, but she didn't open it.

She twisted the key Carraro had given her between her fingers.

Thought about it and shook her head.

She put the notebook in her handbag and promised herself she would check it out at home.

For now, she really needed to go over the police reports on what looked like a pretty big issue: the Badia Polesine massacre, which had all the hallmarks of a couple of rival gangs settling scores.

The sun was casting soft rays on the snowy mountaintops.

After three days of complete rest, her leg hadn't fully healed yet, of course, but the inactivity had been beneficial. She was still limping, but at least she could walk.

It would take some time, but eventually everything would be as it was before. The flesh would repair itself. And slowly, with training and rehabilitation, she would get back in perfect shape.

Mila left her house.

She took a deep breath. She detected the acrid smell of the spruces, the snow glittering in the morning light.

It felt as if she had awakened from a long sleep. An intoxicating feeling of regeneration poured through her body. A light breeze arose. Quite pleasant.

Still ringing in her ears, the words she had heard on the phone, spoken by a male voice with a thick foreign accent: "The boss wants to see you," he had said. "We're waiting for you."

Clearly her snuff clips had impressed someone, enough to give her some hope of joining the BHEG, sooner or later.

She had packed her bag with only the bare necessities.

Her itinerary read: Seven Communities plateau, Pergine, Trento, the Brenner motorway up to the border, then Innsbruck and straight to Garmisch Partenkirchen and Oberammergau. A little over two hundred miles. A four-hour drive in the snow.

All this to get to the Slaughtered Roe Inn at 12 sharp.

As agreed.

It was the perfect day to leave.

She loaded her luggage into the car. She had carefully stuffed the false bottom of the tennis bag with the cash she'd taken from the Galesso twins.

Her blue Ford Focus shone in the morning light.

She locked the door and got in the car. Her leg wasn't bothering her too much.

She revved the engine while the car was still in neutral just to hear the engine roar in anger.

She changed into drive and left with a screech of tyres, the wide treads tearing up the snowy slush as John Kay's low-pitched, resonant tones embark on the opening lyrics of "Born to Be Wild".

# A Conversation

BETWEEN TIM WILLOCKS &
MATTEO STRUKUL

**TIM WILLOCKS:** I am often asked what authors were my greatest influences. I always feel that I should say something like "Nabokov, Dostoyevsky and Faulkner", but the truth is I fell in love with reading – and started writing, as a boy – through pulp fiction: Richard Stark, Mickey Spillane, George G Gilman, and a lot Western authors whose names no one remembers except Joe Lansdale and I. Why do you think that pulp fiction reaches the parts that other forms of literature can't reach? And why is there such a cultural prejudice – which I myself am not immune to, even though I know it's wrong?

**MATTEO STRUKUL:** I agree and I must confess that even my influences are very pulp oriented, thinking about novelists like Chester Himes, Jim Thompson, Charles Willeford, James Crumley, even if I loved authors like Alexandre Dumas, Robert Louis Stevenson, Ernst Theodore Amadeus Hoffman, Friedrich Schiller, Wolfgang Goethe, among others. But even these authors were very popular, you know what I mean?

What I could say about pulp fiction is that maybe it can reach parts and readers more than all other forms of literature because it's profoundly popular. Thinking about pulp magazines like *Amazing Stories* or *Black Mask*, I must confess that there's an enormous amount of characters that have been created thanks to those magazines: The Shadow, Doc Savage, Tarzan, Conan the Barbarian, Fu Manchu, Solomon Kane, Zorro, characters so iconic and powerful that they can capture with just one sentence the reader's attention. I think, in fact, because the novelists who were contributors to those pulp magazines were amazing narrative talents, you know, authors like Robert E Howard, Edgar Rice Burroughs, H Rider Haggard, Fritz Leiber, Philip K Dick, and, more than this, I must confess that – during that period we are talking about, the '30s – even in Italy we had pulp like *Per terra e per mare – Il giornale di avventure e di viaggi*, directed by Emilio Salgari, an amazing Italian novelist, from Verona, who was a real pulp novelist, in fact, who invented characters like Sandokan or Il Corsaro Nero (The Black Corsair). I mean that pulp fiction was so popular because it offered so much amusement and amazing but low-cost stories. And popular literature, in my opinion, is only really popular literature, if it can be mass market distributed.

Professors and academics and intellectuals are so boring and selfish and in fact they use literature like a weapon to divide and create differences between high culture and low culture, between upper and middle class and common people. Fuck them all! Man, it's a shame. I want to be an honest pulp writer, I love mass-market books and cheap literature and as a reader I must confess that I consider you one of my masters even because you are so pulpy and gory when you write your stories... so I hope not to offend you if I say this, but in my opinion what I've written now is an amazing compliment for you, ha ha! This is also the reason why there is this kind of prejudice against pulp fiction: because it's popular and low-cost and honest and... cool. Anyway, I would like to know how much you think movies have influenced pulp and crime fiction today, especially thinking about the fact that you are a novelist and a screenwriter?

**TW:** In the course of arguing the point you just made, the British academic, and novelist, David Lodge asked: "If these kinds of novels 'aren't literature' then what are they?" As he said, an opera is an opera whether it's "grand" or "buffa"; it's all music. I find that the supposedly "higher" forms of literature – or at least of contemporary literature; it's certainly not true of Shakespeare or Homer – seem to find it distasteful to engage with the more primal, visceral themes of life: survival, killing, vengeance, greed, lust, folly and insanity; etc, etc. They don't want to get their pens dirty. But these forces are still alive and well, even if we use bankers and drones to do the job; and with the diversity of 21st century catastrophes roaring towards us, only a fool would assume that those forces won't have their day again, even in the bosom of what is known as civilization. Or as certain American Indians put it: the "civilization disease".

Fiction and the movies have been cross-pollinating each other since cinematography was invented. More than ever the movies steal from literary sources, which is somewhat depressing – at least until they adapt my novels. Movies have had at least as much influence on my writing as novels have. Leone, Peckinpah and Kubrick are my holy trinity. But since we've mentioned the great Chester Himes, and Shakespeare and Bloody Sam, and our excuse is *The Ballad of Mila*, let's talk about decapitation (or even heads in bags). It seems to have been a notable human practice since we found a flint sharp enough to do the job. What's the attraction, both for the human race in general and writers (or at least some of us) in particular?

**MS:** About decapitation… well, I must confess that my favourite movie is *Bring Me the Head of Alfredo Garcia*. I remember when I was sixteen and I watched *The Wild Bunch* with my father. He is a big fan of Peckinpah, by the way. And he said something that sounds like: "Tomorrow we will watch something stronger." The day after we watched that incredible movie with Warren Oates that is a real masterpiece, something so strange and unbelievable that I can't describe. I remember the sequence when

Warren Oates took the ice to refresh the head of Alfredo. Well, there was, and is, something so cruel, merciless, and lurid in that movie, it's like to sniff the devil's smell, you know what I mean. And remembering the words of the Player who was Richard Dreyfuss's character in Tom Stoppard's *Rosencrantz and Guildenstern are Dead* drama, well he said, talking about tragedy at one point, "Well, we can do you blood and love, without the rhetoric, without the love, and we can do all three concurrent or consecutive, but we can't do you love and rhetoric without the blood. Blood is compulsory. They are all blood you see."

So, I think that, as a writer, I must represent violence in its very most extreme dimension, especially if I'm writing about a tragedy and about a vengeance, Mila's vengeance, a woman who had been violated by four men when she was a child. So she is merciless, she is extreme, she is cruel, because cruelty is what remained to her at the end of the story. So, as you said to me one time, if you want to represent violence as a writer, you have to be extreme because violence is always extreme, otherwise you are a liar. I don't know why I'm so familiar with decapitation. In fact, it's a horrible thing that really scares me, but I want to write about feelings, about hatred, about passions, and I want to do it in a very honest way. I'm thinking of Derek Raymond's *I Was Dora Suarez* that was a very disturbing, cruel, shocking novel, or to David Peace's *1974*, or, just to mention an epic work, to the *Nibelungenlied, The Song of the Nibelungs* when Kriemhild swears to take revenge for the murder of her husband and the theft of her treasure... well that is the kind of feeling and atmosphere that I wanted to capture with Mila's feeling... and if you remember at the end of the second part of the epic poem, all the Burgundians are killed in a bloodbath when Kriemhild orders the hall to be burned with the Burgundians inside. So, in the end, I think that I was writing about decapitation because I wanted to express how profoundly horrible and all-consuming a woman's vengeance could be.

And talking about vengeance, a real classic in literature, what do you think about the difference between a man's vengeance and a woman's vengeance?

**TW:** Revenge seems to be a very deep-seated instinct. Taking personal revenge (rather than socially sanctioned revenge via the law) has been forbidden for a very long time – all the great religions disapprove of it, and all legal systems, no doubt because it's a recipe for anarchy. So, why is revenge the core element in such a vast amount of drama from the ancients to this day? We never seem to get tired of it as a theme. I certainly don't. It's hard to beat the excitement and satisfaction of a hero taking to the vengeance road, as Mila does. Even when the moral of the tale is that vengeance is bad – "Dig two graves", etc – it's the vengeance that keeps us hooked.

I recently read some research from Yale University which demonstrated that, when watching a puppet show, babies as young as eight months old prefer characters who punished a "bad" puppet to the characters who treated it with kindness. "That puppet needs to be decapitated!" they gurgle. (They also preferred characters who helped a puppet in difficulty to those who made things worse or did nothing.) This was interpreted in terms of evolutionary psychology (which is all the rage these days, for convincing reasons). Revenge in these terms is a "hard-wired" expression of the need for justice, fairness, right and wrong, if a society is going to survive.

On a more emotional psychological note, I

think revenge is more fundamentally a reaction to humiliation, again as with Mila. If there is no humiliation involved, the same painful or tragic event provokes very different feelings. If a loved one dies of an illness, our house burns down, the bank crashes with all our savings, or we are physically injured by accident or nature, we feel bad in all sorts of ways, but we don't feel vengeful. If someone does these same things to us – murder, arson, theft, assault – it torments us in a very different way. We're humiliated, shamed, insulted – and we want pay-back. It's not the calamity itself, it's the loss of power.

In real life, we almost never get revenge; we very rarely try to take it; the consequences are too grim; we not only understand the "two graves", we are also usually afraid of the person (or institution) who fucked us. I think this is another reason for the great satisfaction that revenge dramas give us. Having wasted a great deal of time on real-life revenge fantasies that never got further than high blood pressure and grinding off fragments of my teeth, I must say I love them. When I come back in my next life, I want to be Lee Marvin in *Point Blank*.

As for *Bring Me the Head of Alfredo Garcia*, it's without doubt a great masterpiece, and possibly the most sophisticated meditation on revenge and humiliation in the whole genre. It even includes a wonderfully vengeful woman.

On that topic – male versus female – I'm not sure what to say. I would guess that the impulse is just as strong, but that violent methods of acting on it are generally less available to women.

I always find writing women characters a greater challenge than writing about men. This seems to me perfectly natural. I'm always afraid I will make them too masculine; and then I fear that my fantasy of what it is to be feminine will be "too feminine", ie based on cultural prejudices and clichés, especially as I like to write characters from the inside. Your central character is a woman. What are your feelings about that challenge?

**MS:** Well, I feel good, and my choice was the best one for me. I think that the reason a woman is the central character of my novel is that I wanted a powerful character that could change and upset the structures and clichés of Italian crime fiction, where always you have a giallo, or a hard boiled male main character like a detective or an inspector. So, in Italian crime fiction women are never, ever protagonists, except for the classical, tired cliché of the femme fatale or the dark lady. Hey, we live in 2013! And it's a shame because – during these years – we've discovered wonderful female characters in pulp and crime fiction and movies, like Luc Besson's Nikita, Quentin Tarantino's Beatrix Kiddo (strongly inspired by the *Lady Snow Blood* manga, in fact), Stieg Larsson's Lisbeth Salander. So, as a writer, I think it would be anachronistic not to have an Italian powerful female character in crime fiction. More than this, a female character offered me interesting perspectives: contradictions, fragility and savageness, sweetness, and rage and, above all, integrity. I think because, in Italy, women have never had power: political power, professional power, social power. So, it's a kind of revenge because of this. I'm just a novelist, so I can't change anything, of course, but I would like to testify that, in my opinion, a woman, today, could do everything she wants, especially today when in Italy we have this social plague called Femicide, the killing of females by males because they are females. Two thousand women were killed by men in the last ten years in Italy. Have you any idea of how many characters like Mila we need? Well, I don't want to say that women have to kill Italian men, of course not, but it's a tragedy and a proof, if proof were needed, that women have to take the power in this stupid, idiot "macho country". So, there were so many reasons to have an Italian woman as a central character for my novels that I can't count all of them. More than this, as a novelist, I was afraid to put something of myself into the novel, and I don't want to make that kind of mistake, and I had a unique opportunity: to write a female character. What a great challenge! And, well, I want to thank my wife, Silvia, because we talked and talked about Mila, and her virtues and vices and the way she talks, the way she fights, the way she cries, everything, so it was amazing and very interesting, and I learned so many things and now I think that the "Mila" character is not too feminine or too masculine. She is just a woman, a killer, a victim, an avenger.

Anyway talking about the tormentor/victim relationship… it's something that's brilliantly told, in my opinion, in your first two novels, *Bad City Blues* and, of course, *Green River Rising*. What do you think – as a novelist and psychiatrist – about this explosive kind of relationship and how powerful and useful could it be to build a disturbing plot and story?

**TW:** I think we all know the basic fear that can be induced simply by asking a question. Who can forget those horrible, adult faces looming over us in childhood and screaming: "Where have you been???", or "What's the capital of Singapore???" Or my own boyhood favourite, combining numerous different branches of philosophy, neuroscience and depth psychology in a single a question that I'm still battling to answer: "Who do you think you are???"

For the Inquisition, and the French legal system of the ancien regime, "The Question" was synonymous with torture. Is it cultural training, or is our fear of the question inherent? It's amazing that such a simple, non-physical, behaviour can be so deeply aggressive. It's certainly a delicate matter in psychiatry. "Do you hear voices?" is enough to set anyone on edge. I originally intended Bad City Blues to be one long conversation, ninety percent dialogue, but I quickly gave in to the irresistible allure of explicit sex and violence.

So let me put you on the rack, Mr Strukul. Why do you think that the people who have just read this book should immediately tell all their friends and family to rush out and buy *The Ballad of Mila*?

**MS:** Good point, good point. Well, what can I say? Maybe, because, in my opinion, to read this book is a little bit like watching a movie. The Ballad of Mila is a fast paced novel, heavily influenced by American authors like Joe R Lansdale, Don Winslow, Victor Gischler, Charlie Huston, Jason Starr, Duane Swierczynski (especially if you think of novels like *The Blonde* or *Severance Package*), and Chuck Wendig. But I have to mention also comic books. Garth Ennis's *The Punisher* and Frank Miller's *Elektra* are major influences for my work and all the novelists who I have mentioned before worked as screenwriters for Marvel or DC Comics or both, with the only exceptions being Winslow and, probably, Wendig. I am a comic book screenwriter too and I was so lucky to work together with Alessandro Vitti, who drew a wonderful three issues arc that I wrote and that had Mila as its main character, and was awarded with an important Italian award. So, I must admit that, especially in this first novel in Mila's on-going series (I'm working on book number three just right now), I was influenced by American pop culture. I loved all the crime stuff of that new generation of novelists who had Lansdale and Winslow as masters, and developed a new fresh way to approach pulp and crime fiction. So, I think that American readers could feel "at home" with *The Ballad of Mila*.

At the same time, there is something different in my novel, I hope, and it is an Italian flavour, because I tried to mix all the tricks and shootings and showdowns and action sequences of American pulp fiction with Italian taste. For this reason, we call this particular, bastard genre here in Italy Sugarpulp, that is, in fact, the pulp with the sugar, which is the most important product of the north-eastern area of Italy. In the beginning of the Twentieth Century, we had, here in the region of Venezia and Padova, the biggest sugar refinery in Europe, so that's the reason why we call this particular genre Sugarpulp, because it's the American pulp mixed with the Italian attitude, landscapes, lands, cities, and crime. In some ways, Sugarpulp is a new brand or genre like Spaghetti westerns once were. I don't want to compare *The Ballad of Mila* to a masterpiece like *A Fistful of Dollars* or *For a Few Dollars More*. I'm not so arrogant or mad. But the idea, the mechanism, the scheme to take something from another place and genre like American pulp fiction and to put some Italian white beet sugar on top is a little bit similar, as the attempt to take the classical western and recreate it in a different way like the Spaghetti western did. But, back to *The Ballad of Mila*, as a reader you could learn about the Spritz, the classical aperitif that you can drink here in Veneto, a cultural heritage of Austro-Hungarian Empire, that occupied our region for a very long time in the Nineteenth Century, or the battle for the territory between the Chinese Mafia and the local gangs, and that's just for starters.

And then you have Mila.

A bombshell: medium height, red dreadlocked hair, green eyes; sheathed in leather trousers and a tight jacket, perfectly highlighting her curves. Breathtakingly hot. But, at the same time, she is lethal, a deadly assassin, a professional killer. Mila's character is also in the tradition of Elektra, Cat Woman, Domino…

For these reasons, I hope that all English language readers would be so generous and curious as to give a chance to *The Ballad of Mila*.

But talking about Spaghetti Westerns, I know that you have a huge admiration for Sergio Leone, Sergio Corbucci, and some of the other Italian directors and authors. Why do you think they are so interesting and inspiring for your work and in general for other crime fiction authors?

**TW:** Sergio Leone was my first true artistic hero, and, dementia permitting, I plan to watch *The Good the Bad & the Ugly* on my deathbed. I, too, have a great father to thank for that. He took me to see the Eastwood trilogy when I was about twelve years old and those remain among the most mind-blowing moments of my life. One is more easily impressed, perhaps, at that age, but considering that *A Fistful of Dollars* is now fifty years-old, it retains a quasi-surrealistic freshness and originality that very few works of art retain and which no contemporary movies can lay claim to. It's hard to remember just how radical those movies were at the time. Needless to say, they were universally trashed by the clever people at the time, as was just about everything by Kubrick and most other great directors. But then the *Times* of London also trashed Beethoven's Ninth on its first performance, so that tells you everything you need to know about reviewers.

I think the great lesson to take from Leone is, on the one hand, to trust your own vision, and on the other, to match classical myths with radical new imagery and themes to create something no one has ever seen before. Which I think is what *The Ballad of Mila* does. The establishment is always fundamentally conservative; that's their nature. Intellectually, they wear carpet slippers and smoke a pipe (strictly tobacco only, which they don't inhale). Leone, like other greats, reached beyond them to the audience. Establishment culture limps along to catch up about a decade or two later, by which time it's all changed again – or should have. These days the grip on the means of production – and mass indoctrination – is so tight that it's much more difficult now to break through. The corporate machines don't like originality. They are happy for us to eat the same swill from the same troughs forever, and technology has been their greatest asset in that process.

So, I think one should always go for the throat and write without fear, before the clock runs out on the arts altogether. Of course, it's ten-to-midnight on far more terrifying clocks than that. Maybe when those chimes strike, the arts will return to some semblance of their former importance. I'm still with Burt Reynolds on that: the machines are going to fail. Or at least fail us.

There's an undercurrent of a sci-fi vibe to

Mila. Perhaps, like the Leone movies, a sense of a parallel universe, something hyper-real, almost uncanny, which is part of the effect. Are you aware of that, or is it an unconscious process? Most of my effects are unconscious – I don't really know what I am doing. I deliberately try not to think too much. How cerebral is your writing process?

**MS:** Talking about Mila, my writing process is totally visceral and compulsive. When I start a Mila novel, I have no synopsis, no plot, nothing, just a logline or something like that and an image, a picture that I have in my mind and that I know I want to tell and describe during the story. Sometimes I need an entire novel only to justify the meaning of that scene, because that scene is so important and seductive and powerful for me and I really need to put that image or sequence into the novel. I think that this is the reason why Mila is, in some way, a character so fresh, hopefully, because she can't make plans or projects or whatever. Of course she is number one as a professional killer, she is disciplined like a soldier, but at the same time she is pure instinct and so you can never know what she will do or think. But, I must also say that, on a different level, there are some other influences or elements that, often, are "working" in the back-office of my brain.

And you are perfectly right! There is a kind of sci-fi vibe in Mila: the glasses, the cameras, things like those. I think that the two main influences that created that kind of vibe are Luc Besson's *Leon* movie (that will be also a main influence for the third Mila's novel) and Duane Swierczynski's *Severance Package* novel, that really blew my brain away when I read it some years ago. It's a wonderful novel so much influenced by comic books, I think, but I have to ask Duane if I'm right, because I'm not sure. Talking about Luc Besson's work, even with *Nikita*, he directed a real masterpiece that form together with *Leon*, in my opinion, a kind of great diptych. I don't know if you have ever watched those two great movies, but there were unforgettable sequences, in fact, that I can't erase from my mind. Like when Gary Oldman ate the pill and was going completely crazy, or, at the end of the movie, in the final shootout, when you have hundreds and hundreds of SWAT with machine-guns who have to kill just one guy.

I love those two Besson movies. They're a main unconscious influence for my work and all those kind of vibes and martial obsessions that you can taste in *The Ballad of Mila* and even in its sequel *Black Queen – the Justice of Mila*. But, sometimes I have to plan something like a synopsis or a plot, especially if I have to write something different like my last historical thriller. I researched and studied so much that, in the end, the story was perfectly completed and well-defined in my mind, but I know this doesn't work with Mila. She's like a beast sometimes: she has no plans, no dreams, no projects, she is pure fury, you know what I mean? And it's fine to me because I know that, in this way, I can be honest with my character and with my readers.

Integrity and faith in your story and characters: this is the best way to write a good story, I mean.

Do you agree? About integrity and loyalty to the story and characters? What do you think about that? Because it seems to me that this is very important for you, as a novelist, and for your stories. You do not seem that kind of writer who wants to please his readers…

**TW:** Well, I wish I could please more readers, but it's hard to make characters do what they don't want to do. I'm not sure readers care all that much about the author, or that they should. My loyalty as a reader is more to the characters. I can think of plenty of writers whose work I liked only in part, ie I loved some, or even only one, of their novels and not others, or only one of their characters. For instance, Mickey Spillane's Mike Hammer brought me an immense amount of joy, but his other series characters left no impression on me. DH Lawrence said, "Never trust the artist, trust the tale". There are far too many stories in which the characters act out-of-character in order to fulfil the larger message that the author wants to convey. All that "hero's journey" stuff has become a bit tedious, too, the "character arc", and so forth – the hero as student, learning some great truth (usually a very obvious one) about himself. It's certainly become a disease in Hollywood.

In fact, the great series characters never fundamentally change at all. Mike Hammer would rather pull his own teeth out, and eat them with the entrails of dead communists, than alter his rabid machismo. James Bond never changed. Parker never changed. We didn't want them to. Real people only change by tiny increments, and that's usually for biological reasons – ie age and its associated neuro-endocrine decline – rather than because of some moral epiphany. It takes truly great drama to pull off a real character arc, and that's rare. What was that great Conrad line in *Heart of Darkness*?

"Droll thing life is – that mysterious arrangement of merciless logic for a futile purpose. The most you can hope from it is some knowledge of yourself – that comes too late – a crop of inextinguishable regrets."

Wow. Imagine being able to write a line like that. But Mila is a series character. Do you see any fundamental changes coming for her?

**MS:** An incredible line: breathless! Hey, this is *Heart of Darkness*! Well, after this, what can I say? Yes Mila is a series character… I think that integrity for her is the most important thing, but integrity, for her, is something that works in a very particular way. She is a predator, that's for sure, and she is "damaged goods", like she said. She can't accept herself for what she is, because someone made her ten years ago into what she is now, and she doesn't like what she sees. So, she is full of regrets and rage and pain and sweetness and all these feelings and bloods and souls are trying to stay together in just one woman. I love what she represents for me. She is not only a character, of course, she is a woman in flesh and blood, you know what I mean? And I remember that it was a little bit strange when, after the first novel, the readers asked me if Mila would have fallen in love with someone, and I must confess that I said, "No." And for that reason, I wrote a second book that was tougher and harder and more bitter than the first one. *Black Queen* was strongly influenced by more UK authors: Derek Raymond, Adrian McKinty, Allan Guthrie, and as I probably told you, an author named Tim Willocks. There is also the German tradition: Friedrich Schiller, Novalis, Theodor Storm, Ernst TA Hoffman, Heinrich von Kleist, but the point was that I wanted Mila to be able to face the evil side of men, not for a personal vengeance, but to protect another woman. That topic was really intriguing for me.

After that, in her third novel, I think she will deserve a little bit of tenderness, but a little bit, not more than that, and she will protect a black child from traffickers, contractors and slavers. Together with that small child she will recover and collect something she had lost. But all these kind of changes are necessary for her to leave her life and path of blood and glory, because Mila is blood and glory and not because I want that for her. Maybe one day she will fall in love, but not today. Personally I don't like it so much when a series character is the same every time. I like that it's coherent, that's for sure, but what I need and like, as a reader and also as a novelist, is that she or he will grow up and discover new feelings and reactions and things that belong to her or him. I don't like so much to read the same old story in every episode or novel. That's the reason why I loved Cicero Grimes and Jefferson as characters in novels like *Bad City Blues* and *Bloodstained Kings*, you know what I mean. Probably what I love are epics and sagas more than series. What I want is not only a new quest or adventure for my character, I think that I need more than this.

And you? What do you think about the difference between series and epics and sagas? I'm asking because, in fact, even your second novel – in the Tannhauser series – is completely different, in my opinion, from the first one: darker, stronger, faster than the first one, in my opinion, do you agree?

**TW:** I'd say that, apropos my above comment, the "epic" or "saga" – grand tales of heroes, usually historical – are the classical embodiments, or even the literary blueprints, of "the hero's journey". There is some evolution in the nature of the character; it's more of a chronicle of a life, or part of a life. The traditional series character – Bond, Parker, Travis McGee – doesn't change, but that's part of the appeal – they're like an old friend that you can rely on. They never get older; they don't change their attitudes or methods. This makes them more predictable, but that's part of the pleasure they give us. Perhaps it goes back to the pleasure of childhood when we loved to hear or read the same story dozens of times. "Read it again!" Some research suggests that we do actually get more satisfaction if we know how a story ends – which is why some people read the end of a book first. It makes one wonder why one should go to the trouble of creating suspense, though even if one does there is always someone who will smugly declare that they saw it coming from page thirty. Another reason not to try to please people, as you can never please everyone.

I always feel an obligation to go beyond where I have been before in a new novel, though I am not sure it is wise. Like everyone else, I have often had the experience of being disappointed by something new from an artist I love. Why wasn't *Blood Money* as good as *Rain Dogs*? Why wasn't *The Aviator* as good as *Goodfellas*? Where is *Blood Meridian II*? What's wrong with these people? Gimme another masterpiece, now! But of course it's ridiculous; inhuman even. To make even one great work is almost impossible. Six is a miracle. But twelve? Twenty? The fine arts are an interesting – or puzzling – exception. I am no expert in these matters, but it seems that while we don't hesitate to identify at least some work by even such towering figures as Shakespeare or Beethoven as "minor", virtually everything splashed on a canvas by Picasso or Monet is, by definition, "a masterpiece". I know that used to mean simply, "a work by a master", but that's not what we mean. There are a handful who never fell below that level – Leone, Kubrick – but they tend to have smaller outputs.

*The Twelve Children of Paris* has a different tone and pace to *The Religion* because it was a very different place and situation. It had to be darker and more intense, though the pacing is in some ways an illusion created by the timescale of the story. As Aristotle pointed out, a story taking place over months or years will inevitably feel "slower" than one taking place in hours or days, no matter how "intense" the writing or events. Film has developed various techniques for cheating this – *Goodfellas* uses them all, brilliantly – but the manipulation of time in film is easier because time is part of the very fabric of the medium. *Twelve Children* is more like *High Noon* or *24*; it's a 36-hour story that probably takes about 36 hours to read. Most of my books take that approach – I like the intensity it provides. When there are time gaps, I always wonder what the hell the characters are doing. Sleeping? Talking about football? Why isn't there something important going on? Even though one leaves out the boring bits, the reader knows unconsciously that they are there.

The 21st Century is moving faster than anyone can keep track of. Everyone is clinging to the roof of the train hoping they won't fall off – except for the elites, who are inside it; but even they, if they have any intelligence, are waiting for the train to hurtle off the tracks, or hit the various trains coming in the opposite direction. Literature has always tackled its own present, tried to illuminate it even if subliminally. How can the novel – how can we – approach our own present, given that it is changing at such speed? Even the most prescient writers, like William Gibson, are outdated almost by the time their novel is published. Technology is moving faster than the literary imagination – which is no surprise as technology is imagination and, unlike the writer in his isolated pit, the techies are working in vast, highly-paid teams in gleaming laboratories all over the world. So how do we write about now? Can we? Has the novel outlived its time? Are we heading the way of opera and theatre – into the museum of culture?

**MS:** Personally, I don't think so. Of course technology has changed prices, distribution, marketing strategies, but not the most important thing: a good tale is a good tale. I have no doubt about this and it doesn't matter if you sell that tale in eBook, audiobook, paperback or hardcover, because I'm sure that the story is the central point, even today. And also powerful characters, razor plot, fast-paced action, a unique atmosphere, profoundly and originally described and written, are all key elements. You can write original and strong stories for movies and videogames, you can call them screenplays or screenwriting or plot or synopsis or whatever you want, but everything must start with a great tale, a great story. Love and war, passion and hatred, history and fantasy, are immortal and enduring and represent our hearts and feelings and souls for ever. The point is: how good is your story?

More than this, I think that through technology, we will have more readers today than in the past, and maybe thanks to technology, they could give a chance to a new author for a very small amount of money, and if that novelist is a good one and they love him, then maybe they could buy a hardcover edition of one or more or all of his books. So, I'm optimistic, and I'm very grateful to Exhibit A and Angry Robot, because they understood perfectly how important it is today to offer different editions and formats of the same story. We have new devices like Kindle and Nook or whatever, and we have to use them to help build and create a close relationship between an author and his readers, today more than ever.

*With massive thanks to Tim Willocks*

# Acknowledgments

For this spectacular English-language edition I would like to thank His Majesty Allan Guthrie, an extraordinary author and the King of all British Editors; Marco Piva-Dittrich, the Grand Bailiff of Translations and a very close friend – practically a brother; and Emlyn Rees, the best Editor-in-Chief I could ever dream of having. Huge thanks to all the team at Exhibit A and Angry Robot. And then thanks to Lyda Patitucci, who directed the cinematic teaser *Mila in Bloodstained Delta,* and to Melissa Iannace, who took the amazing cover picture.

Tim Willocks gave me the huge honour of discussing Mila with me at the end of the novel.

It was wonderful: for me Tim, just like Allan, is a role model and a guiding light. Thanks to Victor Gischler for the fantastic intro. He is my personal hero and a huge inspiration for my work. Many thanks also to Linwood Barclay and Joe R Lansdale. And to Marina Alessandra Marzotto... she knows why, ha ha.

To all of you who are reading this English language version – please give the killer with the red dreadlocks a chance: you won't regret it. To booksellers, promoters, journalists and bloggers who are kind enough to give Mila some exposure: I hope to meet you, wherever you are, to thank you in person.

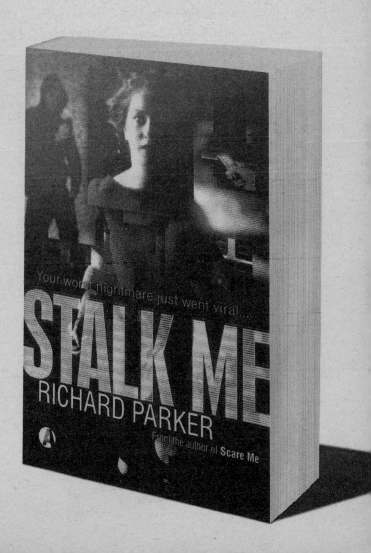

"Gripping from the first page to last."
Winston Groom, author of *Forrest Gump*

# Robert Bailey

## The Professor
### A LEGAL THRILLER

Sometimes winning
means everything

**In 1976, four boys walked into the jungle.
Only three came out alive.**

DAN O'SHEA
A Detective John Lynch Chicago Thriller

GREED

A gripping psychological thriller about
love and betrayal.

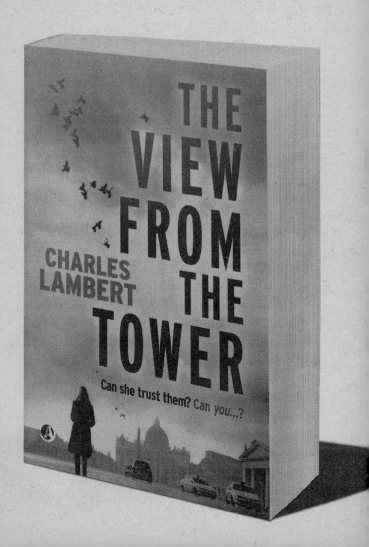

THE
VIEW
FROM
THE
TOWER

CHARLES
LAMBERT

Can she trust them? Can you...?